# DATE DUE

PRINTED IN U.S.A.

# SKYJACKED

# SKYJACKED

## PAUL GRIFFIN

SCHOLASTIC PRESS / NEW YORK

Library of Congress Cataloging-in-Publication Data

Names: Griffin, Paul, 1966- author.
Title: Skyjacked / Paul Griffin.
Description: First edition. | New York, NY : Scholastic Press, 2019. |
  Summary: Five teenagers from the elite Hartwell Academy are on their way back to New York from an end-of-summer camping trip in Idaho when they realize that something has gone wrong; one of them has become violently ill, and their private plane has apparently been hijacked and is headed in the wrong direction— and even if they can somehow break into the cockpit and manage to overpower the hijacker, they have no idea how to fly the plane, much less land it.
Identifiers: LCCN 2018053889 (print) | LCCN 2018059150 (ebook) |
  ISBN 9781338048032 (ebook) | ISBN 9781338047417 (hardcover)
Subjects: LCSH: Hijacking of aircraft—Juvenile fiction. | Survival—Juvenile fiction. | Interpersonal relations—Juvenile fiction. | Adventure stories. | CYAC: Hijacking of aircraft—Fiction. | Survival—Fiction. | Interpersonal relations—Fiction. | Adventure and adventurers—Fiction. | GSAFD: Suspense fiction. | LCGFT: Action and adventure fiction. | Thrillers (Fiction)
Classification: LCC PZ7.G8813594 (ebook) | LCC PZ7.G8813594 Sk 2019 (print) | DDC 813.6 [Fic]—dc23

10 9 8 7 6 5 4 3 2 1                    19 20 21 22 23

Printed in the U.S.A. 37
First edition, August 2019

Book design by Yaffa Jaskoll

For Risa and Ani

## THE PASSENGERS

**Cassie Ando**: *the daredevil, her family owns the plane*

**Brandon Singh**: *the serious one, Cassie's best friend*

**Tim Cuddy**: *the football hero, boyfriend of Emily*

**Emily Alarcón**: *the big-hearted one, might have a crush on Jay*

**Jay Rhee**: *the new guy, on scholarship to the private high school they all attend*

**Reeva Powell**: *the chaperone, hard to read*

## THE PILOTS

**Tony Blake**: *longtime pilot for Cassie's family*

**Nick Sokolov**: *Tony's usual copilot, out sick the day of the hijacking*

**Sofia Palma**: *Nick's replacement, new to piloting*

## THE INTERN

**Michelle Okolo**: *eager to prove herself to General Landry at the National Air Traffic Investigation Center (NATIC)*

# Prologue

## MICHELLE

*July 28, 1:34 p.m. Eastern Time (ET)*

*Coltsville, Virginia, NATIC*

Michelle Okolo always made sure she was at her desk, ready to work, twenty minutes before the start of her 2:00 p.m. to 10:00 p.m. shift. She didn't need to be so early. The first six weeks of the internship had been uneventful. Technically her title was research assistant, but mostly she poured coffee.

"Okolo, I'm looking into an empty mug," a senior research analyst said before Michelle could take off her backpack.

"Yes, sir," Michelle replied. She hurried to the coffee station. How being a waitron was going to help her get into the United States Air Force Academy, she had no idea.

Sixteen years old, she was a rising senior. She'd read about NATIC in the *US Air Force Journal*, the monthly magazine that kept coming to the apartment even though her father had been killed four years ago in a test flight. If the local air traffic control center had known about the sudden windstorm that day, the director would have recommended that USAF Captain Reginald Okolo divert course. But the storm was just outside the control center's primary area of responsibility. The information about the wind came in a few seconds too late.

NATIC was formed about a year after her dad died, with the purpose of obtaining and sharing critical weather information in real time. It also kept everybody up to speed about air-related terrorism threats. The chance to serve at NATIC—even if she was mostly serving coffee—thrilled Michelle.

She eyed the Big Board, a screen fifty feet wide and thirty feet tall. It tracked every flight in US airspace. There were thousands of dots, most of them blue, which meant the planes were on course. A few dots were orange, the planes straying from their designated flight paths, usually due to wind. The orange dots always turned blue within a minute or so, after ATC—air traffic control—radioed the plane to correct its position. There was one now, over New Jersey: orange to blue, everything fine.

Michelle delivered the coffee, settled in at her desk, and hoped her eyelid would stop twitching. She had been clicking around on

Instagram way past bedtime. And then she sat up straight, her focus on the bottom of the Big Board.

There was one other color a dot could be: red. That would be a plane off course and not responding to air traffic control. Michelle had never seen a red dot, until now.

It was crossing into Texas from Mexico.

*Blant-blant-blant*—an alarm went off in the auditorium.

Michelle's unit, the research team, scrambled to a long table in front of the Big Board with their laptops. One of the researchers wore a headset. He called across the auditorium to Major Serrano, Michelle's boss, whose desk gave her a prime view of the Big Board. "It's a mayday," the researcher said. "Multiple bird strikes, starboard engine blown, port struggling to maintain power. ETC at present altitude is five minutes."

*ETC?* Michelle's stomach constricted and turned cold as she remembered what it meant: estimated time to crash.

"Michelle," Major Serrano said. "This is an all-hands deal. Hit the keys."

"Me?"

Major Serrano frowned. "Hey, you know what we do here, right? Get on your computer and find me a place where I can land that plane."

"Yes, ma'am," Michelle said. She'd memorized the emergency protocol manuals, but she'd never expected to have to use them—not in her lowly position as a research assistant, and definitely not the crash-landing protocol. What was the first step again?

*Water.* Right. Step one: Find water. She had to find water within five minutes' flying time of the plane's current position. Four minutes now. How fast was the plane moving?

She tapped up the flight information. "Six hundred and forty miles per hour," she whispered to herself. She ran the numbers: At six hundred and forty miles per sixty minutes, the plane, with four minutes until impact—less than four minutes—would have to find water within forty-two miles. She launched her graphing app and plotted a semicircle with a forty-mile radius over her map of south Texas.

Within the semicircle there was no body of water, at least not any big enough to accommodate a landing plane.

Step two in the protocol: Find an out-of-use landing strip.

No go.

Step three: Locate a desolate area, one without infrastructure like train tracks or power lines.

There was none. The landscape was suburban sprawl and industrial waste storage.

The only option left was awful: Find the area with the lowest population density.

"I need coordinates, gang," Major Serrano called out.

Michelle looked at the Big Board. The plane was on course to hit ground in Kappock, Texas, population 241,000 and evenly spread out within the plane's landing range.

Wherever the plane landed people were going to die.

She zoomed in on her map but scanning the entire area for population density and flat terrain at the same time would take minutes she didn't have, even with multiple statistics and topography apps running.

There was only one thing to do now: Log onto Facebook.

She tapped up her page and ran a search with the words *Kappock Texas highway expressway freeway.*

Several hundred feeds came up with matches. After scanning a few posts, mostly complaints about traffic, Michelle figured out that the area's main expressway was due east of Kappock's commercial district. She pulled it up on her map. It was seven lanes with a wide, grassy median.

"Anybody?" Major Serrano called out to her team. She turned to Michelle. "Okolo?"

Michelle hesitated.

"Michelle, now or never, give me what you got."

"Route 46, Major. I mean 64. No, wait, yeah, 64."

Major Serrano called out to her assistant, "Get Kappock ATC to raise the alerts, radio, text, all of it. I need that highway cleared."

"Eastbound or westbound?" the assistant said.

Major Serrano nodded at Michelle. "Which is it, Okolo?"

How could this be possible, Michelle wondered, that the selection of the plane's crash site had fallen to her, a low-level intern?

She looked at her map screen, then the Big Board, which had zoomed in on the red dot, so much bigger now, brighter, blinking faster as the dying plane lost altitude. In two minutes it would be tearing up the highway, but in which direction?

The eastbound highway was three lanes wide, the westbound four. The plane's wingspan was 197 feet. If it landed toward the westbound's outside emergency lane, the wing would barely overlap the eastbound lanes. Yes, wider had to be better.

"Westbound?" Michelle said.

"Is that an answer or a question?" Major Serrano said.

"West—westbound, ma'am."

"The westbound lane is heading into the city, Okolo."

"Ma'am?" Why was the major *smiling*? Why wasn't she calling in the order to clear the highway?

"It's morning rush hour, Michelle. The westbound lane where you put that 787? It's a parking lot. You just killed eighteen hundred commuters."

The research team surrounded her cubicle.

The *blant-blant-blant* stopped. *Time* stopped, or seemed to. One wrong decision—*her* decision—could kill eighteen hundred people? At least eighteen hundred. No way that 787 would hold together after it hit all those cars and trucks.

The Big Board returned to normal status, most of the dots blue, maybe three orange dots, no red.

"It . . . crashed?" Michelle gulped, but the knot high up in her throat wasn't going anywhere.

"It was a simulation," Major Serrano said.

"What do you mean? Like, a *trick*?"

"We call it an emergency preparedness drill. You're furious, I know."

"I'm not, ma'am," Michelle said, but she *was* all right. *Oh* how she was. She'd barely been able to find the words. She couldn't keep from shaking, from *glaring* at the major.

"I'm sorry, kiddo, but you have to taste the fear before you can learn how to swallow it. The fear that whatever you do, whatever decision you make, people will die. It doesn't happen a lot. Maybe once every five years. But toward the end of your thirty-plus year career, when you're sitting in my chair, you will, at some point, more than likely have to make the call."

"Hey, at least you put the plane on the highway," one of the senior research analysts said. She turned to Major Serrano. "Remember that kid who wanted to land it in the amusement park on a beautiful Saturday afternoon?"

"Not a big roller coaster fan, that one," Major Serrano said.

"Chin up, Okolo," another researcher said. "Everybody fails the Kappock nightmare."

Michelle forced herself to nod. *And everybody doesn't get into the US Air Force Academy*, she thought.

"I'm looking into an empty mug," Major Serrano said. "You'll be all right, Michelle. We live and learn, right? We live to fight another day."

"Yes, ma'am," Michelle said, taking the mug. She almost made it to the coffee station before she cursed herself. She'd just told a pilot to land a wide-body 787 head-on into rush hour traffic. *Way to go, Michelle*, she thought. *Dad would be so proud.*

She looked up to the mezzanine of glass-walled offices that overlooked the Big Board.

General Landry, the founder of NATIC and its highest-ranking official, was at her desk, on the phone. She was expressionless, as usual. She rarely came down to the floor, where the research team worked, and when she did, she was all business. She'd have a quiet word with Major Serrano, and then she was gone, no time for chitchat.

A letter of recommendation from General Landry was a guaranteed appointment to the USAFA, one of the most selective schools in the world. The government paid for everything: tuition, room, board, travel stipends. Upon graduation you were guaranteed lifelong employment in service to your country. *Not to mention the opportunity to honor your dead father*, Michelle thought, stirring sugar into the major's coffee.

Well, there was no chance for a letter from General Landry

now, after Michelle had totally blown it with the Kappock sim. Even Major Serrano, who had taken Michelle under her wing, would probably think twice before she could recommend Michelle for a spot in the academy. The air force's applicant wish list most definitely did not include a mediocre barista who made terrible decisions under pressure.

# JAY

*One month later, the last Friday of August, 9:55 a.m. Mountain Time (MT)*

*Crabbe's Fork, south-central Idaho*

Their sneakers were Nike custom jobs and New Balance. His were knockoffs from Payless. But here they were, all together, the five of them, in the middle of Crabbe's Fork National Forest, standing at the edge of a cliff. Jay hung back a bit as Cassie squatted to check the slackline that spanned the canyon.

It wasn't that the Hartwell kids weren't nice—they were. Okay, Tim had been a little cold to him once or twice, but Cassie, Brandon, and especially Emily were all right. Emily had pretty much adopted Jay at the welcome session for new transfer students last month. She'd invited him on this trip to Idaho with Cassie and her friends.

"One last summer blast," she'd said it would be, before the start of sophomore year.

His mother forced him to go. Didn't he want to make new friends? Not really. He just couldn't see how he'd have much in common with these kids who'd been going to Hartwell since kindergarten. Their parents had gone there too.

The Hartwell Academy English Department had put a bunch of F. Scott Fitzgerald stories on the summer reading list. All these dandies in tuxedos, mansions on the beach. Jay delivered store circulars and lived in city-owned housing. Did he really need to know about the so-called troubles of privileged white folks in the 1920s? But there was one thing good old F. Scott wrote that made a lot of sense. *"Let me tell you about the very rich. They are different from you and me. They possess and enjoy early, and it does something to them."* Understanding these people was a constant challenge. Like, for instance, why was Cassie staring down into the valley floor with an unsettling grin?

"How far a fall do you think that is, Timbo?" Cassie said.

*Timbo* was six four, two fifty easy, already a starter on the varsity football team, noseguard, at fifteen years old. He dropped a rock over the edge of the cliff and counted, "One, two, three, four, five," before the echo of the *click-click-crack* made it up the cliff. "I'll tell you exactly how far down that is," he said. "It's exactly *far.*"

"Well done, Tim," Emily said, patting his very wide back.

"It's a half mile anyway," Brandon said.

"Then I better not fall," Cassie said. She hopped onto the slackline and danced like a ballerina. She wore a safety cuff on her ankle, but still.

"Casserole, it's official: You're insane," Emily said. "Really, you have to pirouette? Cass, what are you doing? Don't!"

"Cassie, no!" Tim said.

She unclipped her safety cuff and cartwheeled in slow motion along the slackline.

"Cass, I'm gonna kill you!" The words weren't out of Emily's mouth when Cassie slipped.

She just barely grabbed the line with both hands. She looked down, seemingly more fascinated than terrified. "You guys, this is so beautiful. I'm floating."

Maybe that's what she said. Jay couldn't be sure with all the screaming Tim and Emily were doing. His pulse rate must have doubled, he was pretty sure, the blood whooshing against his eardrums, or was that the very strong wind?

Brandon grabbed the line and made his way, hand over hand, toward Cassie. "No, Brand," Cassie said. "Go back! I'm fine!"

She wasn't anywhere near fine. Her grip broke, and now she was hanging on with one hand. Just four fingers on the line now . . . three . . . and then she fell.

Brandon snatched her wrist. He hung upside down from the slackline by his legs. He'd been smart enough to wear a safety cuff, but Jay didn't think it would be able to bear his weight and Cassie's if Brandon's legs slipped from the line. And they did.

Now they both hung by Brandon's cuff string. It looked like a string anyway, practically fishing wire in Jay's eyes, not that he'd ever been fishing. That would change soon, once he and the others hiked down into the river filled with jags of granite to retrieve Cassie's body, or what would be left of it. Brandon wouldn't be able to maintain his grip on her for much longer. His arm was starting to shake.

"Brand, let go!" Cassie said. She tried to peel his hand from hers.

It was definite now: Money made you stupid. Jay Rhee from Flushing, Queens, was not going down with these crazy rich kids from the Upper East Side. But then why was he moving toward the edge of the cliff, toward the slackline?

Cassie's sweaty hand slipped through Brandon's, and she fell.

# BRANDON

*9:58 a.m. MT*

*Crabbe's Fork, Idaho*

The digital display morphed to 9:59. That would be the time of death.

Brandon's wristwatch glowed in the foreground as he hung upside down from the slackline and watched Cassie become small, smaller, shrinking in less than a second to a blue dot in her jeans and cobalt-colored shirt—and then a burst of red.

The parachute exploded from the low-profile backpack she'd been wearing.

Brandon heard Emily curse Cassie for being a lunatic. Tim, always Cassie's cheerleader, howled his approval. Brandon felt both ways: He was angry with Cassie and admired her at the same time. He understood why she had a habit of daring fate.

It was just how she was wired.

Brandon's father had been the same way. He'd told Brandon that sometimes you had to do the things that scared you. If you died in that pursuit, so be it, just as long as you died with a pure heart. Mr. Singh had been ranked one of the top trauma surgeons in New York when he volunteered for a tour of duty with Doctors Without Borders—a mission advertised as extremely dangerous. He was at work on a patient, the death report said, when a friendly fire airstrike mistakenly blew up the mobile hospital on the Iraq-Syria border.

Cassie's chute was a paraglider. She steered it dangerously close to the sharp-edged rubble that lined the canyon wall.

Cassie liked to tease Death a little too much, Brandon thought, but what could he do to change that? They'd been friends too long for him not to know she was on a mission of her own: to live each moment like it could be the last. Maybe it wasn't such a bad way to live.

Cassie was about to crash into the rocks when she veered toward the water and a gentle waist-high landing.

They met up with Cassie two hours later along the riverbank. Emily kept proclaiming how furious she was with Cassie—for five minutes. Trying to stay mad at Cassie Ando was impossible. Her smile was ridiculous, huge and a little lopsided with a dimple in her left cheek, and before you knew it you were grinning too.

The hike back to camp was noisy with everybody gabbing away—everybody except the new kid, Jay. Brandon liked him and his quiet way. He patted Jay's shoulder. Jay flinched.

"How you doing after Cass's little joke back there?" Brandon said.

"Some joke."

"Seriously, Cassafras, I'll never stop being mad at you," Emily said.

"I apologized how many times now, Em? And *you're* gonna hold a grudge? Not likely."

"You could have killed Brandon and Jay."

"Notice how she omits me," Tim said. "Friends, I know who I am, and no way was I going out there on that slackline, not even if my mom was dangling. All I have to do is live to twenty-two, and my trust fund opens wide."

"My hero," Em said.

Brandon understood where Tim was coming from. He didn't admire Tim's taking the easy way out, but taking insane risks was, well, insane.

Jay's phone rang.

"So much for getting back to nature," Emily said. "The phone companies even have the so-called remote areas of the parks covered, lest we miss any Snaps of somebody making herself look like a cat."

"It's my mom," Jay said. He fell back to talk with her. They'd checked in with each other twice a day since the beginning of the trip. With Jay away, Mrs. Rhee'd had to walk home alone from her health aid shift that ended at midnight.

Brandon wondered what that would be like, having to stay up late to walk your mom home and then waking up at five to deliver store circulars before school.

Cassie nudged Brandon to give Jay some privacy.

"I probably would've snapped the slackline anyway," Tim said. He was laughing.

"It isn't funny," Em said. She hung back to wait for Jay.

# 3

# EMILY

## 12:11 p.m. MT

*Crabbe's Fork, Idaho*

Jay finished his call and fell into step with Emily as they headed toward camp a bit behind the others.

"You've had a pretty bad time this week, I think," Emily said.

"Nah, it's been great," Jay said a little too cheerfully, too quickly, the way you do when you're trying to fake your way through an awkward conversation, hoping the other person won't press you for more, like *What was your favorite part of the trip?* "It's just that I feel a little weird being out of the city. But thank you for inviting me and all."

"I'd say we're not really like this, but we are. Crazy, I mean. Annoying."

"Nah," Jay said.

"*Nah,*" she teased.

"Seriously, I appreciate how nice you've been and everything. I mean it: I had a good time."

"Wow, you are a spectacularly terrible liar."

He actually cracked a smile, and then it was gone, but whoa, she'd gotten him to grin! Mostly he brooded, and that was okay too. His brooding was authentic. He wasn't trying to look like a cool loner, like a lot of boys at Hartwell did. He actually *was* a cool loner.

"You'll need somebody to look out for you when school starts," she said. "You know, to keep you from falling in with the wrong crowd."

"A wrong crowd at Hartwell? Like anybody there's gonna throw away their ticket to Princeton?"

"Well, I'm appointing myself your guardian," she said.

"Yeah? Okay, I guess it can't hurt. Thanks, Emily."

That was the first time he'd said her name. It sounded nice the way he said it, softly.

Sweaty from the hike, Emily felt a tingle in the skin on her arms.

When they got back to camp, Jay joined Brandon and Tim as they started to pack up the boys' tent. Cassie pulled Emily into the girls'. "He's totally into you," Cass said. "And you're into him."

"Cassafras, as I believe your actions have proved this morning

20

and yet again, you are certifiable. We are one hundred percent completely and only friends."

"You're falling in love with him. You just don't know it yet. But I think Tim does. As we were walking back, he kept looking over his shoulder to see where you and Jay were. He was a little gloomy there."

"He's such a baby. But he's *my* baby, be sure of that."

"Whatever you say, Em," Cassie said.

Reeva, the kids' chaperone and one of Cassie's dad's security team, leaned into the tent. "We should get a move on if we want to make that flight," she said.

"Thanks, Reeva," Emily said.

After Reeva left, Cassie frowned.

"You've had bad vibes on her the whole week," Emily said. "What's up with you?"

"She makes me uneasy. She's cold."

"She's new, right? Give her a chance. She's just being professional."

They got to work with the others, packing up camp. Reeva helped tuck the gear into the back of one of the SUV limos. Tim pointed to the gun strapped into a low profile holster at the small of Reeva's back. "No way I could take a shot with that before we head off, like at a tree or something?" he said.

"No way," Reeva said with a relaxed smile.

"Tim, seriously, you really think Reeva can let you play around with her gun?" Emily said. "Besides, why would you want to shoot a poor tree?"

"A rock, then," Tim said. "Look at her now. Emmers of the rolling eyes. Relax. It's just I've never shot a gun before. Reeva, you ever worry someone's gonna come up from behind and grab it?"

Reeva's smile seemed forced now. "Let's get the rest of the gear in here ASAP, before we're late for the airport."

"I think they'll wait for us," Tim said. "That's how it goes when you have your own plane."

"Yeah, but we don't have to be jerks about it and mess up the flight schedules for everybody else," Emily said. "You know, the other planes carrying people who aren't you."

Jay came up with the last of the packs.

"So, Jay, you're gonna miss this place, huh?" Reeva said.

Jay looked toward the canyon, the one he might have died in if Cassie hadn't fallen just as he was going out onto the slackline without a safety cuff to help Brandon. "It was . . . interesting," he said.

"Did you check in with your mom?" Reeva said.

"Yeah, thanks, you?"

Reeva nodded, and there it was again, that forced smile. Her mom had early onset Parkinson's disease. Emily found out about that one when Reeva had to take a call in the limo, on the way out to Crabbe's Fork. Reeva was one of her mother's primary caretakers.

Emily couldn't understand why Cassie didn't like Reeva. She'd come on the trip even though it clearly meant having to find someone to take care of her mom. She'd been laid back too. She didn't insist on going along on the last hike with the group after Cassie asked her if she wouldn't mind staying back at the camp. Emily had thought that was so rude, to exclude Reeva. But then Emily didn't know that Cassie planned to cartwheel off the slackline. Reeva never would have let her get away with that, and Reeva was the only one who had any control over Cassie.

Being friends with Cassie was always exciting, but it could be a job too. Like now, did she have to be giving Reeva a dirty look? Emily pushed Cassie toward the SUV.

Jay got the door for Reeva and then held it for Emily, but she was riding in the other limo with Tim.

Tim was inside already, playing a game on his phone—a game for little kids. The player was an ogre who had to pick flowers from a field and give them to a fairy princess. If the ogre gave her pretty enough flowers, she turned him into a duke or something.

"My prince," she said. "You're so cute."

"Sure," Tim said. He looked over his shoulder toward the other limo, at Jay.

"Hey," she said, turning his head so he had to look at her. "I was just trying to include him. Starting at a new school has to be scary enough, but especially before sophomore year, when everybody knows everybody else already, right?"

"No, I know," Tim said. "He's okay. He is. It's just, I feel a little . . ."

"A little what?"

"I don't know."

"Look." She pointed to his phone screen. The princess surveyed the flowers the ogre had brought her. A dialogue bubble popped up over the ogre's head: DO YOU LIKE MY FLOWERS?

The princess looked sad. I'M AFRAID THEY'RE NOT PRETTY ENOUGH. YOU'LL JUST HAVE TO KEEP TRYING.

## 4

# TIM
## 5:49 p.m. MT
*Hollow Brim, southeast Idaho, near the Utah-Wyoming border*

The driver nodded to Tim by way of the rearview mirror. "You're a sophomore, you said? In college?"

"High school," Tim said.

"Big for your age."

Tim smiled politely, but he'd been hearing that one for as long as he could remember.

"You get the chance to play any sports out there in New York City?" the driver said.

"Football."

"Yup, I figured. Gonna play for the NFL, then?"

"You bet," Tim said, but he didn't know what he wanted to do. His dad had it all figured out, though. Harvard for college, never mind that with Tim's grades he didn't deserve to go there. But when Dad gives a school four million dollars, they overlook a few bad marks. After the Big H he'd go work for his father's company, selling financial instruments, whatever those were. Yes, Tim Cuddy was set for life. So then why was he . . . what? He felt off-kilter.

"I went to the top of the Empire State Building once," the limousine driver said. The SUV cruised past the entrance to the municipal airport, toward the smaller terminal where the private planes waited.

"Amazing up there on the observation deck, right?" Tim said, doing his best to sound friendly despite his down mood. Normally he wouldn't have minded that the driver wanted to make conversation, but Cassie's ballerina routine on the slackline had shaken Tim. He'd frozen when Brandon hadn't. Then Jay had to get in there, ready to step out, no safety cuff even, making Tim look so much worse.

"You must go up there all the time, living in the city and all."

"Now and again," Tim said. He'd actually never been to the top of the Empire State Building.

"You ever worry they're going to do it again?" the driver said. "Knock down another skyscraper? On the TV they were saying an attack is imminent."

Tim nodded, but they were *always* saying an attack was

imminent, and it never happened, at least not to you or anybody you knew anyway. He opened the window, hoping the noise of the highway would be enough of a hint that he wasn't up for a conversation about terrorism right now.

The blast of air woke Em. She settled back into the nook between Tim's arm and his massive chest. "The guy on TV said we're up into the red alert now," the driver said. "No, I wouldn't want to be visiting that Empire State Building today."


Tim loved flying in Cassie's dad's plane. There weren't any security lines at the private airport terminal, and skycaps took care of your carry-on bags. Tim noticed Jay was shaking a little as he handed over his bag.

"You're acting like this is your first time getting onto a plane," he said.

"Second," Jay said.

"You serious? The trip out here, that was your first time?"

"I almost lost it when we hit the turbulence."

"Turbulence?" Tim said a little too gleefully. "Relax, Jay-dawg, the weather's perfect the whole way back. I checked."

"I saw thunderstorms in the south."

"We're not going that way. It's due east for us, clear skies straight through to New York."

They met up with Brandon on the other side of security. The

cart filled with the camping gear had been wheeled up to the belly of Cassie's dad's private jet and left unattended. The boys loaded the gear into the luggage bay until the skycap ran up.

"I've got this, gentlemen," she said. "Head on into the plane now, please."

Just before he ducked into the jet, Tim looked back.

The skycap had opened one of the tent cases. A TSA officer with a bomb-sniffing dog came to check it, but the dog didn't find anything of interest.

# 5

# CASSIE
## 6:52 p.m. MT
*Hollow Brim, Idaho*

Cassie cruised the airport gift shop. She knew she'd blown it with her stunt out on the slackline. She'd meant to scare everybody—mission accomplished there—but who would have thought Brandon would go out to try and save her?

Well, anybody who knew Brandon, and who knew him better than Cassie?

Friends since pre-K, they'd been through a lot together: her parents' divorce, his father's death, his mother's depression. Brandon had been all in for a career as a doctor, the kind who'd work in an underserved area, just like his dad. Now Brand just took it day by day, made few plans, no promises. He made an exception

29

to the no-promises rule when it came to the one thing that really mattered to him: friendship. He'd always been there for Cassie, and she repaid him by dragging him out onto that stupid slackline?

And she felt *really* bad about Jay. He was so sweet, holding doors and making sure everybody else had taken from the communal dinner pot before he dug in.

What if Jay had come out onto the line and fallen? What would his mother do then?

Cassie thumbed a climbing magazine. She was feeling really blue, and she couldn't let the others see her this way. She had to be Happy Casserole, the one who makes you laugh so hard you cry.

Poor Tim really had been crying. His face was the last thing she saw before she jerked her hand free from Brandon's and let herself fall. Of course, later Tim had played the whole thing off with, "No way was I going out there," a riff on his go-to self-serving rich kid routine, which seemed less outrageous and even less funny as the years went by. Sometimes he seemed to act like a jerk to spite himself, to make people not like him. *Why?* she used to wonder. Lately she'd begun to understand. You look for other people to feel about you the way you feel about yourself, to confirm your growing understanding that, despite all your money, your opportunities, you're lost. Being rich put you in some serious danger of becoming a drone.

Cassie Ando wasn't going that route. She was going to live hard and fast, and die young if it came to that. She wasn't suicidal, but after what happened to Brandon's dad, she knew that there were no guarantees. You didn't get any points for hitting all the right marks, for making your parents happy, for living the life they lived. Her father worked so hard she rarely saw him. When she did, he looked dazed and somehow on edge at the same time, afraid to slow down enough to take in a moment with his daughter, as if he really should be working, growing the stupid company for her to run someday.

Well, no way was she working for Ando Chemical Inc.

She was more likely to work *against* the company, maybe as a lawyer representing people whose air had been polluted thanks to the lobbyists the chemical companies hired to jam their agendas through Congress. She hadn't figured out how to tell her dad this yet, but he must have known. How could he not after she formed an environmental activism group in school last year?

Her mom was just as crazed, sitting on who knew how many boards of directors for this nonprofit and that charity. She ran around so much, the only time she could grab a meal with Cassie was outside the apartment, at whatever restaurant happened to be closest to Mom's next appointment. Yet Cassie didn't dare complain because she had gobs of money. The poor-little-rich-girl routine and the self-pity thing in general were beyond off-putting.

Em came up and slung her arm over Cassie's shoulder, gazing around the gift shop with her. "You okay?"

"Totally," Cassie said.

"Not," Em said.

"Look." Cassie pointed to a stuffed Appaloosa horse, Idaho's state animal. "For Tony," she said.

"He'll love it, especially the rhinestone tiara."

Over Em's shoulder, on TV, a most wanted terrorist promised to unleash bedlam.

"Howdy, neighhhhbor." Cassie leaned the horse's head into the cockpit and made a whinnying sound. Em had come along to say hi to Tony.

Tony looked up from the flight-programming screen and scratched the horse's forehead. "Does she prefer apples or carrots?" He had both in the Tupperware he kept near the control panel. He was a health food nut.

"She prefers you." Cassie handed the horse to Tony.

"Aw, Cass, that's really sweet," Tony said. "Thank you. My goddaughter will love it."

"Em, take a picture of us, and I'll text it to her."

"Use my phone," Tony offered.

"Where's Nick?" Cassie grinned for Emily and the camera.

"Poor guy had to call in sick. You look a little pale yourself there, kid. Here, have some apple, get that blood sugar up."

"Granny Smith, my fave." Cassie took a slice.

"Emily, here, bring these outside and share them with the gang."

Emily was reaching for the Tupperware when a Nerf football hit her in the back of the head, and she forgot all about the apple slices. "Excuse me while I go murder Tim," she said.

Cassie dug into the Tupperware. "Nick never gets sick," she said, her mouth full of apple. "What, is it like the flu or something?"

"Food poisoning. He was pretty sure he was done vomiting, but he couldn't get out of bed. Said he'll stay out here another day at the hotel and sleep it off, catch a flight back to New York in time for your dad's trip to Kyoto."

"He's going *again*? I swear he just got back."

"Now, Cass," Tony said.

Cassie cut him off. "I know, I know, 'Money never stops moving, so why should I?'" she said, reciting Dad's mantra. "So, what, you're flying solo today?"

"I would if the FAA'd let me. It's their job to worry what would happen if I had a heart attack midflight, but you'd know how to land us, right?" He winked.

Tony and Nick had let Cassie hang out in the cockpit since she was a little kid. Tony was low-key about everything to the point it was unnerving. Like the time they had to fly through a lightning storm that had seemingly come from nowhere, Tony sat back nonchalantly, one hand on the steering control, humming some rock ballad. Cassie had watched him land the plane so many times by now, she was actually pretty sure she would have no problem getting the plane onto the runway without too many bumps. "Bet you I could."

"I *know* you could," Tony said. "You'll have to wait for your chance, though. The staffing agency sent us a replacement. She's top-rated. I double-checked."

"Why? You're worried about her?"

"Was. You'll see." He tried not to smile.

"What, is she like a narcoleptic or something?"

"Shh, here she is." Tony cleared his throat. "Cass, this is Sophie."

"Sofia," the substitute copilot said, stepping into the cockpit, staring at the stuffed Appaloosa horse.

"Sofia, this is my dear friend Cassie Ando, the boss's daughter."

"Oh, yes, hi." Sofia offered her hand nervously to Cassie. She was tiny, about a foot shorter than Cassie, though Cass was five-ten. Sofia looked about twelve years old. No wonder Tony had double-checked her rating.

"Hi." Cassie shook Sofia's hand. Her skin was cold, and was she trembling?

Sofia gave Cassie a smile that seemed forced, then said to Tony, "I checked the supplemental oxygen tanks, sir. Two thousand PSI."

"Really, Sofia, you don't have to call me sir."

"The luggage hold is screwed shut tight. I watched them seal it."

"Cass, why don't you make a little room there and let Sofia get to her seat. Sofia, you ever fly the B550 before?"

"Yes."

"Good, then I'll let you do all the work today."

Cassie hoped she didn't look as worried as Sofia did. Then again, Tony would never let anything go wrong.

Reeva leaned into the cockpit. "Tony, ready to do our thing?"

"It's a family flight today, Reeva. I don't think we have to worry."

"The protocol is the protocol," Reeva said.

Cassie wanted to roll her eyes. She followed Reeva and Tony out of the cockpit, to the gun safe inside the coatroom. "Man, Sofia's really tiny," Cassie said.

"This way she can't overpower me when she tries to hijack the plane, right, Reeva?"

Reeva's lip twitched. "Why would you even say something like that, Tony? You're aware the country's on high alert?"

Cassie was so close to telling Reeva to chill out.

Reeva turned away so she couldn't see Tony key his pin code into the safe's touchpad. Tony tapped the numbers, not caring if Cassie or Reeva or anybody saw, and then he made room for Reeva. "All yours," he said.

"Would you mind turning around, Tony, with your back to the safe?" Reeva said.

Tony wasn't looking anyway. He was heading back to the cockpit.

The idea was that anybody who wanted access to the safe—and the gun—would have to know both codes. Only the pilot

35

and security agent could get in there, and only together. This kind of security precaution made sense when Dad rented the plane to people he didn't know, but really, one of Cassie's friends a terrorist? Cassie knew it was Reeva's job to be alert and maybe even suspicious, but Tony had been with the Andos for years. Reeva had been with the family only a few weeks.

"Cassie, take your seat, please," Reeva said.

"Yes, ma'am." She saluted and left Reeva to enter in her supersecret code.

# 6

## MICHELLE
### *9:35 p.m. ET (7:35 p.m. MT)*
*Coltsville, Virginia, NATIC*

Major Serrano and the NATIC research team hadn't given up on Michelle after her tragic failure in Texas, even if it was hypothetical. Instead they'd assigned her roles in some pretty solid projects—nothing on the level of the Kappock simulation but important nonetheless.

Mostly she checked passenger lists of planes that exhibited suspicious flight patterns or sudden altitude changes. With the major's permission and her research security clearance, Michelle could tap into the Center's FBI and NSA intel pools, but she preferred trying social media first. That's what 90 percent of the FBI's databases were anyway, open-source information from Twitter, Facebook, Instagram, Snapchat.

Getting the info directly from the platform feeds had a downside: The intelligence agencies hadn't analyzed it yet. The upside was the information was raw and therefore pure. Michelle's job was to determine which passengers had grievances so big they might want to hijack or crash a plane. On the bigger flights, there were always two or three or sometimes more people who were haters or very strident in their political opinions, but of course none of these people ever acted on their feelings. The pilot always corrected the plane's flight path or followed ATC's directions. Still, it was good to have the passenger information on hand.

At first some of the older researchers scoffed at Michelle's use of social media, but they couldn't argue with the results. Michelle Okolo often found what the team needed before anyone else. She never gloated, though. She offered the information humbly, quietly, in the hope she'd earn the senior staff's respect. Even now, almost at the end of her internship, she wasn't sure how people felt about her. Today was her second-to-last day at NATIC, and she'd begun to clean out her desk.

Major Serrano was approaching Michelle's cubicle.

Michelle wondered when or if she should ask the major for a recommendation. Without that letter, Michelle's chances of an appointment to the academy were the same as any other candidate's with her resume, which was to say less than 10 percent.

"I'll need you to stand by at your desk for a bit," the major said. "Don't go anywhere, all right?"

"Yes, ma'am."

The threat assessment window at the bottom of Michelle's display began to blink red. *Great*, Michelle thought. *Another stress test.*

# JAY

*7:45 p.m. MT*

*In the Ando family's airborne B550 SE-11 jet*

The takeoff was so smooth Jay almost didn't feel the plane leave the runway. He was surprised, but he shouldn't have been. He'd looked up the plane's specs online, back in New York, before he had to board it for the first time.

The B550 SE-11, or Barracuda 550 Special Edition #11, was known to be a luxurious ride. Okay, so with a cruising speed of 520 mph, it wasn't the fastest plane, but from takeoff in Hollow Brim, Idaho, to touchdown at the private airport in Teterboro, New Jersey, would be a none-too-shabby four hours. In the safety category the B550 ranked first in its class. The autopilot software was so advanced the plane could land itself, even on water. The plane manufacturer didn't need to advertise this feature, as far as Jay was concerned. It was in no way reassuring.

The plane had room for thirty seats, but Cassie's dad had it set up with just ten, recliners that folded out into beds, as Brandon and Cassie were demonstrating.

There was a full-size dining table and a gaming area built around a wall-size TV. Tim was playing a creepy game where a monster plucks weeds and tries to trade them with this elfy-looking lady for who knew what.

The kitchenette was stocked with ridiculous amounts of gourmet food, candy, designer soda, and ice cream. The windows had touchscreens built into them so you could darken the glass to dial down the glare, which Jay did. The cabin was pure luxury. So why was he on edge? There wasn't any turbulence, yet something wasn't quite right.

Emily brought him a chamomile tea. "It'll calm your stomach," she said.

Tim plunked down in the recliner next to Jay with a sigh. He'd made himself a parfait with heaps of chocolate. "Seriously, how does anybody fly commercial?"

"He thinks it's funny to play the disgustingly spoiled snob," Cassie said.

"I am a disgustingly spoiled snob," Tim said. "Want some?" He held a spoonful of gooey chocolate flecked with red sprinkles under Jay's nose.

Jay clutched his barf bag.

Brandon pushed Tim's arm away. "Jay, let's hit a video game. It'll clear your mind."

"Clear it of what?" Jay said. "The fact we're hurtling through the tropopause if not the stratosphere at five hundred and some miles an hour?"

"The *tropopause*?" Tim said. "Clearly your full-ride scholarship is for astrophysics or whatever. Hey, I bet he's the best science student in all of New York. Dude, you could have gone to Stuy even, also for free. I mean, so what it's a public; the Ivies take in a bunch of those Stuy kids."

"Tim, are you serious?" Brandon said. "Eat your ice cream before I make you wear it."

"Who ever heard of the tropopause?" Tim said.

"Me," Cassie said at the same time Emily said, "We all did— those of us who weren't napping and drooling their way through earth science." She was glaring at Tim.

"It's for baseball," Jay said to Tim. He was eager to change the subject. "I pitch."

"You should try out for football," Tim said. "No, I mean it. Our quarterback graduated last year. We need an arm. Bro, I was just messing with you, okay? I didn't mean to give you a hard time."

"Then don't," Em said.

Tim snapped. "Why don't you two just make out already?"

"Tim," Cassie said. "Just, stop talking, okay?"

Em's cheeks had turned red. Jay felt worse for her than for himself.

Tim was as flushed as Em, then the color drained from his face, and he looked queasy, maybe even sorry. "I'm being an idiot," he said. "I don't think I slept the whole week. That inflatable mattress felt more like a yoga mat. I'm out of my mind. I'm sorry, Jay-dawg. I am, really." He offered his hand for a shake.

Jay wanted to ask Tim not to call him *dawg*, but what was the point? He shook Tim's hand. "No problem," he said.

"Em, seriously, I'm an idiot." He looked like he was about to cry. Emily brushed his hair out of his eyes, but then he swung his recliner away to look out the window.

"Okay, no sadness allowed on this plane," Cassie said. "Or do I need to do my thoroughly awesome, oh-so-realistic simulated fart song?"

"No, you absolutely do *not*," Brandon said. "Cass, please, I'm begging."

"Ew, don't, Cass!" Em said.

"Do it, Cass!" Tim said, suddenly cheered up.

She licked her hand, tucked it into her armpit, and cranked out "Oh Susanna." Tim sang along and threw in a real fart.

"Stop the plane," Em said. "I want to get off, blehk! Jay, I swear we're not all this disgusting."

But Jay was laughing too. He peered over the seats to check Reeva's reaction.

Reeva sat up near the coatroom. She didn't pay any attention to the gang, her seat swiveled away so Jay saw her in profile. Deep into her phone screen, she tapped away at a text, it seemed like, which was weird, because Tony had said the plane's internet was down, and Jay didn't think there would be any cell service this high up.

Tony came over the PA system with, *"Friends, welcome to Flight 21, departing from Hollow Brim, set to land a bit after one thirty a.m. in Teterboro, with the two-hour time jump. We've just about reached our cruising altitude of thirty-seven thousand feet. We're looking good for a smooth flight all the way into the New York metro area, so sit back and enjoy the ride."*

Jay was going to try to do exactly that. He just had to darken his window some more. The glare was . . .

The glare. That was it, the thing that was so wrong.

Jay, seated on the left side of the plane, pointed out his window.

"What's up?" Brandon said.

"The sun," Jay said.

"So?"

"Why are we seeing it?" Jay said.

"Um, because it hasn't *set* yet?" Tim said.

"We're supposed to be flying east, right?" Jay said. "If the sun is in the southwest, we should only be able to see it out the *right*-side windows. My window here is facing north, supposedly. Unless I'm hallucinating, that big orange ball there to the north is the sun."

"Except the sun is in the south," Em said.

"So your window is facing south," Tim said. "So what?"

"It means we're flying west," Brandon said.

"Last time I checked, New York is east," Em said.

"We're probably just looping around," Brandon said. "I mean, it would have to be that, right?"

"Are you asking *me*?" Jay said.

"Casserole?" Em said.

"I'm sure that's exactly what it is," Cassie said. She didn't seem even slightly sure. She looked over her shoulder at Reeva.

Reeva was perfectly still, hands folded in her lap, no expression. Now she was wearing sunglasses. Her head was angled toward the sun-filled window.

"You all need to chill," Tim said. "Tony said sit back and enjoy the flight. Amen." He pulled down his sunglasses to block out the rays, which most definitely were shining directly into his eyes as he looked out the window, toward what had to be the southwest, Jay was sure of it.

# 8

## CASSIE
### 7:50 p.m. MT
*In the B550, somewhere over central Idaho*

Cassie headed for the cockpit.

"What's up, Cassie?" Reeva said.

"Could you take off your sunglasses, please?"

Reeva did. "Everything okay?"

"We're heading west."

"Northwest, actually," Reeva said. "Probably some air traffic control situation."

"It's just that things are a little different today," Cassie said. "You know, with the substitute pilot."

"I know."

"You're not worried?"

"Cassie, I expect the plane will turn soon, and then we'll be heading east."

"I'm just gonna check to see if Tony's okay."

"Let's wait a couple of minutes, to see if the plane makes a turn. If it doesn't—"

"Reeva, I don't mean to be disrespectful, but if something bad is happening up there—"

"Why would you think that? The plane isn't making any wild dips. Tony didn't activate the emergency call button."

"The cockpit door," Cassie said. "It's shut."

"So? That's the protocol."

"Tony always leaves it open anyway, so I can hang out up there, once we're airborne. You remember on the way out here? He kept the door open the whole flight."

"He shouldn't have. I didn't push him about it, but I told myself that next time I'd have to say something. He's with a new pilot, so he's following the protocols—that's good. Cassie, wait."

Cassie kept heading for the cockpit door. She pulled the door lever.

It wouldn't budge.

Reeva was right behind her now.

"He locked it," Cassie said.

"That's the proto—"

Cassie banged on the door. "Tony?"

Tony clicked in over the intercom. *"What's up, Cass?"*

Cassie clicked the intercom. "Why'd you lock the door?"

*"Now, Cass, we don't want our friend Sophie here to get the impression we don't run a tight ship. We always bolt the door, right? I'm sorry, Sofia, I meant."*

Cassie clicked and said, "Why are we heading northwest?"

*"A bad weather report came up on the screen shortly after take-off. We're getting the heck out of its way. You head on back to the TV there, pick out a couple of movies, and we'll be on the ground in Teterboro before you finish the second one."*

"So, you're, you know, okay?"

Tony laughed. *"You're sweet, Cass. We're good up here, all right? Head on back and get a couple of those pizzas going for team Hartwell."*

Cassie nodded to Reeva. "He's okay."

Reeva smiled. She clicked the intercom now. "Tony, how much longer do you think we're going to have to divert to avoid the storm? I ask because I didn't see anything but clear skies on the weather report, and that was just before we left."

*"It's a windstorm, friend, no precipitation. It won't show up in a conventional weather report. I'm looking at it right here on my screen. 'Severe updrafts reported throughout southern Idaho, extending east into Wyoming.' Soon as ATC gives me the all clear, I'll swing this bird around toward home, okay? Thanks."* He clicked off.

Reeva put her hand on Cassie's shoulder and guided her, a little more than gently, into the pass-through hallway between the entry-way and the coatroom, back into the passenger cabin.

"Everything okay?" Em said.

"It's just some freaky wind thing."

Tim stirred from sleep. "Mommy, are we there yet?"

"Let's have some pizza," Cass said, not wanting any herself. She felt a little light-headed. Hunger usually accompanied the dizziness, but right now the idea of food made her nauseous.

"Meatball for me," Tim said.

"*No* meatball for him," Em said.

"Em, give me a hand," Cassie said.

# 9

## EMILY
### 7:56 p.m. MT
*In the B550*

Emily was getting up to help Cassie with the pizza when the plane shuddered. She grabbed Jay's hand to steady herself but let go when she caught Tim eyeing their clenched hands.

"Strap into your seat belts, gang," Reeva said calmly.

Em felt herself being pushed back into her seat. The plane was gaining altitude rapidly.

"Reeva," Cassie said, "what if Sofia did something to Tony?"

Cass did not look good. She got woozy if she went too long without eating, but this was different, Em could tell. Cassie's lips were bluish, her eyes watery.

"Are we supposed to be flying so high?" Jay said, looking out the window. "I can see the earth's curve."

"Forty thousand feet is as high as we're supposed to go," Cassie said. "Tony once told me higher than that is mostly for military planes."

"We're at forty-one thousand feet, plus," Brandon said. He held up his phone. His altitude app said 41,550 feet, then 41,650 . . .

"This is fun," Tim said. "I feel like we're being whipped up a roller coaster track."

The PA clicked on. *"Buckle up, friends,"* Tony said. *"Crazy wind out there today. We're gonna climb over it. Should be on top of this thing in a minute or so. Hang out in your seats until I give you the all clear. Thanks."* He clicked off.

"Cass, it's okay. See?" Emily held Cassie's hand. It was clammy, cold.

"I'll get you some orange juice," Brandon said.

"Jay, give me that barf bag," Cassie said.

"I never figured the slackline walker would be the first one to hurl in a little turbulence," Tim said. "Whoa, Cass, I was just kidding. She's really gonna puke."

## 10

## MICHELLE
*9:58 p.m. ET (7:58 p.m. MT)*
*Coltsville, Virginia, NATIC*

Michelle's coworkers sang, "For she's a jolly good intern, for she's a jolly good intern." They came bearing a farewell sheet cake.

"Make that wish, Michelle," Major Serrano said.

Michelle closed her eyes and wished that somehow, someway if not somewhere, her dad was watching her, and that he was proud of her for what she was trying to accomplish with her life.

She also wished for that letter of recommendation.

When Michelle opened her eyes to blow out the candles, everybody was hurrying away from her cubicle. On the Big Board, a red circle pulsed around a small orange dot heading northwest over Idaho, toward a patch of airspace known as RFD-NW6-10, or restricted flight deck 6 of the northwest United States, altitude level 10. It extended from central Idaho, northward to the Canadian border and westward into northeastern Oregon, then Washington State, angling toward Seattle, to the coast.

That airspace was for military planes only. Signal jammers blocked radar and prevented spy satellites from peeking in. If a pilot turned off her GPS, the plane was as good as—

"Gone," Major Serrano said, as if reading Michelle's mind. The orange dot disappeared from the Big Board.

# 11

## BRANDON

### 8:02 p.m. MT (7:02 p.m. PT)

*In the B550, crossing into the Pacific Time Zone at the Idaho-Oregon border*

Cassie had finished throwing up and looked a lot better. *Okay, not a lot*, Brandon thought.

Reeva brought the medical kit. She put a digital thermometer into Cassie's ear.

"How hot am I?" Cassie said, winking.

Brandon looked at the thermometer: 96.2. She was 2.6 degrees *colder* than normal?

That was worse than 2.6 degrees too high. Low temperature was a sign of coming shock.

"Do you mind if I try that again?" Brandon said to Reeva.

She gave him the thermometer.

"Is it bad, Brand?" Cass said.

"No, Cass, it's fine. Just want to double-check."

"We've been flying northwest for more than half an hour now," Em said.

*And too high*, Brandon thought. His altitude app had crashed at forty-five thousand feet, but he'd felt the plane continue to climb.

"What if Cass is right?" Em said. "What if Sofia has a gun to Tony's head, and he's just acting calm, saying what she's telling him to say?"

"No way she could get a gun into the plane," Brandon said.

"Reeva did."

"I'm on a list that clears me to carry a firearm," Reeva said. "And as security detailed to this flight, I would have been informed of any requests to bring additional weapons on board."

"Maybe she pepper sprayed him with one of those minicanisters that look like lipstick," Jay said. "Those things are no joke."

"How do *you* know?" Tim said.

"I got one for my mom. Hey, I just tried my phone, and I get no signal. But my phone's garbage. Did you guys try yours?"

"Where you going, Reeva?" Em said.

"To tell Tony Cassie's sick."

"If he's still alive," Em said.

"You guys seriously think this tiny little Sofia chick broke Tony's neck with a karate chop while he wasn't looking or whatever?" Tim said. "The dude said there's a storm. We're flying around it. We'll be fine."

Cassie reached for Brandon's arm, then doubled over and threw up bile. This time there was blood in it.

Brandon held Cassie's hair back from her face to keep it from sweeping through the puddle. He rubbed her back gently, the way he would have for any of his friends.

*Friends.*

Just friends.

He and Cassie had talked about it once, making their relationship something more. In the end they decided nothing could be more than what they already had, that being *in* love with each other might jeopardize their love *for* each other. Now Brandon regretted that they hadn't tried.

Cassie's eyes were swelling shut.

The blood in her vomit, the swelling in her lips, her face—what was provoking this reaction? You can't fix something when you don't know what's causing it.

He had to fix this, to keep Cassie from slipping away.

"Cass, stay with me, okay?"

"I'm not going anywhere, Brand," Cassie said.

One of the things that Brandon loved most about Cassie was that she was a really bad liar.

# EMILY
## 7:11 p.m. PT
### *In the B550*

Emily wiped the spit from Cassie's mouth with a headrest towel.

"Do you think it's food poisoning?" Emily said.

"With the swelling, it has to be an allergic reaction," Brandon said.

"Is she gonna die?" Tim said.

"*Tim*," Emily said.

"She's going to be fine," Brandon said.

Brandon, Emily knew, was a good liar. He was calm on the outside, but he had a lot of stuff churning down deep. A lot of loss.

"Look at her lips," Tim said. "They're so puffed up they might pop."

"Cass, what are your allergies?" Brandon said. "I know about the peanuts, but how about medications?"

"Penicillin, aspirin, ibuprofen. I'm supposed to avoid the kind with the sleep aid in it. Either way, I haven't had any."

"So you're allergic to narcotics, things like morphine?"

"She just told you she hasn't had any," Tim said.

"Maybe she only thinks she hasn't," Brandon said.

Now Emily was feeling sick. Was Brandon suggesting that Cassie had been poisoned?

Cassie's skin was blotchy, flushed around the eyes, pale around her mouth. Emily put her palm to Cassie's forehead. It was clammy, cool—no, cold.

"Cass, the main thing is, do you feel like your throat's closing up?" Brandon said.

Cass shook no. "It's scratchy, but it's not getting worse."

"Right," Brandon said. "Then whatever it is that's making this happen, it's probably not something that'll—"

"Choke me to death?" Cassie said. She put her hands around her throat and acted like she was choking.

"So not funny, Cassafras," Emily said.

"Dude, do you puke *bloody froth* when you're having an allergic reaction?" Tim said. "I don't think so."

"Stop talking about it." Cass pushed herself out of her seat, toward the bathroom, retching on the way. She stumbled, and Jay caught her before she fell. He helped her into the bathroom.

Em followed them in. Cassie bent over the sink and dry heaved. She turned on the cold water and put her hands under the faucet. Her fingers were puffy like cooked hot dogs.

"Wait," she said. She turned her hands so they were palms up. She stared at them.

"What?" Em said.

"Did you shake hands with Sofia?" Cass said.

"No," Emily said. "You're thinking that's how she transferred it to you, the . . ."

"Poison, you want to say," Cass said. "It has to be poison. If it was viral, we'd all have it, including Sofia."

"If it's poison, and she got it into you by way of a handshake, wouldn't she be poisoned too?" Em said.

"Maybe she built up a resistance to it," Cassie said, her voice hoarse. "Or maybe she just put it on her palm long enough to shake hands with me and then wiped it off. Her hand was sweaty when I shook it, but maybe it wasn't sweat. Jay, you didn't shake her hand, did you?"

"No."

"Go check if the others did."

Jay left.

"We need to get into the cockpit, Em," Cassie said.

"What, like knock down the cockpit door and overwhelm Sofia?" Emily said.

"Or kill her," Cass said. "We may have to. Who knows what she did to Tony. She's not just going to surrender. We have to storm the cockpit and take her out and take over the flight controls before she puts the plane into a nosedive. Why are you looking at me that way, Em?"

"It can't be a suicide mission," Emily said. "It doesn't make any sense. If she wanted to crash a plane and kill as many people as possible, she would have hijacked a much bigger plane."

Jay was back. "Then maybe it's for the money," he said. "All your parents will pay huge ransoms. None of the others shook hands with Sofia. Cassie, Sofia would need an inside connection to pull this off. The regular copilot—what's his name again?"

"Nick," Cassie said. "And no way is he in on this."

"Then why'd he call in sick?"

Cass shook her head. "Nick has been flying with my family for years. He's the greatest guy. It's Reeva."

"Nah," Jay said.

"I appreciate the vote of confidence, Jay," Reeva said, standing in the bathroom doorway. "Cassie, I'm sorry to hear of your lack of faith in me." She reached into her jacket pocket.

## JAY

**7:16 p.m. PT**

*In the B550*

Reeva pulled out her phone and tapped the screen.

"What are you doing?" Cassie said.

"I'm texting your parents' phone numbers to my boss, so he can relay them to the FBI if this thing really is a ransom situation."

"But how are you able to text?" Cassie said. "I can't get any bars on my phone."

"My phone's military grade, with direct satellite linkage. Tony didn't answer when I knocked on the door to tell him you're sick."

Jay had to acknowledge that he was more than afraid now. He was a step away from full-out panic, maybe a half step.

"Reeva, can I see your phone?" Cassie said.

"Why?"

"I want to be sure you're actually texting my dad's head of security."

"I see. Okay, you know what? Here you are, Cassie." Reeva gave Cassie the phone. "You'll find I sent word that you're ill, and we're not sure why. You'll see I reported we've been heading in the wrong direction for more than forty-five minutes, and that Tony didn't respond when I knocked on the cockpit door."

Cassie and Em read.

"Satisfied?" Reeva said.

Her phone buzzed in Cassie's hand. Em read the incoming text. "It's from Rochelle Monahan," she said. "Shelly, Cass. That's her, right? Your dad's head of security? She texted back '10-4, 10-6.' What does 10-6 mean?"

"It means stand by," Reeva said. "Stay calm. Wait for further instruction."

Cassie gave Reeva a nasty squint. "How do we know you're not just texting Sofia, and she's pretending to be Shelly?"

"I guess you don't, Cassie. I don't know what I did to lose your trust, if I ever had it. If I can do anything to reassure you, let me know. Meanwhile, you should lie down before you fall down. You're quivering. Emily, may I have my phone, please?"

"I didn't mean to doubt you, Reeva." Em handed over the phone. "I'm sorry."

"You don't need to be sorry. You're upset, and you're looking for answers. I am too." She said that last bit to Cassie.

Cassie either didn't hear Reeva or didn't want to. She splashed water on her lips, and she didn't apologize.

"I'll see if I can find something to warm you up," Reeva said.

Jay followed her to the food service area. She was calm, almost too calm. Unlike Cassie, Jay didn't suspect Reeva of being up to no good, but she was holding back something. "Do you really think it's a ransom situation, Reeva? Or a suicide mission?"

"I think if it was a suicide mission, the plane would have crashed by now."

Tim was in the kitchenette, putting a pizza in the microwave. "I have to eat when I get nervous, or I start hurling," he said. "I know, it makes no sense, but stuffing my stomach calms it."

"Where's Brandon?" Jay said.

"Thinking," Tim said.

"*Thinking?*"

"Sort of meditating, I guess. He said he had to slow everything down to think clearly. Typical Brand."

"Yeah," Jay said, except he didn't know what was typical for Brandon or any of them, and now he was probably going to die with them.

Reeva opened the medical cabinet. There were blankets and two medium-size oxygen tanks. One of them had a breathing mask fitted to it. Reeva took it from the cabinet.

"You guys need any help?" Tim said.

"You hang out up front with Brandon," Reeva said. "We're good."

*Exactly*, Jay thought. Reeva was good, never mind what Cassie thought.

## MICHELLE
### 10:29 p.m. ET (7:29 p.m. PT)
*Coltsville, Virginia, NATIC*

The room buzzed with more and more people. Satellite images flashed across the Big Board. The tech guys zoomed in on anything that looked like aircraft. "That's not a plane," one of them said.

"What is that, a hawk?" another said. "Hold on, your camera is zoomed in at a five-hundred-foot altitude. Take it up to fifty thousand."

There hadn't been so much as a blip from the plane since it had disappeared from the screen twenty-eight minutes earlier. Nothing like this had happened all summer. The whole thing was a little suspicious, coming on Michelle's second-to-last day.

"Major, seriously, you can tell me: Is this another simulation, or is this real-world?"

Major Serrano nodded toward the observation deck that overlooked the Big Board. General Christine Landry was settling into her chair, studying an iPad her assistant handed her.

"Does that answer your question?" Major Serrano said.

A real-world code red situation? Michelle tasted bitterness in the back of her mouth. Her salivary glands were working hard to keep her mouth from going dry. Her back ached like she'd been kidney-punched. She swore she could feel her adrenal glands squeezing the adrenaline into her bloodstream. This code red deal was scary, and if she was being honest with herself, it was also really exciting.

"Okay, what do we have so far?" the general said.

Her assistant rattled off the information. The plane had gone offline twenty-nine minutes ago in RFD-NW6-10, which meant the plane had either crashed or turned off its GPS.

"Have we tried to make contact?" the general said.

"We don't have the call sign yet, ma'am," the assistant said.

"All senior staff mobilized?"

"Yes, ma'am."

The general scanned the room and the whereabouts of personnel. She hit Michelle with a hard stare—at least it felt hard, almost a glare. "Who are you again?" the general said, though they had never been introduced. In fact, those were the first words the general had directed Michelle's way the whole summer.

Michelle panicked. She couldn't remember her own name.

"This is Michelle Okolo, our intern," Major Serrano said.

"Great. Ms. Okolo, would you please get me a very tall, very strong coffee, milk no sugar?" She didn't wait for Michelle to answer and instead turned to her assistant. "How's the weather up there?"

"Perfect," the assistant said. "No winds to speak of. You couldn't dream up a better day to fly."

Michelle tried not to run to the coffee machine. *Just be cool*, she told herself. This was horrible, this missing plane situation, but it was also an opportunity. If Michelle could get in on this and contribute some decent research, enough to impress the general, then at the very least Michelle could get a letter of recommendation from Major Serrano.

Michelle poured the coffee through the grinds a second time to make it super strong. She added the skim milk—but no sugar—and walked quickly through the Big Board room to the general's desk.

The general took the coffee and barely nodded thanks. She sipped it as she studied her iPad, and then . . .

General Christine Landry spit the coffee into the cup. "Skim milk," she said.

"Yes, ma'am?" Michelle said.

"I take my milk full strength, Ms. Okolo." The general didn't seem at all upset, yet she wasn't thrilled either.

"Sorry, ma'am. I, I'm—"

"This is a game of nerves, Ms. Okolo," the general said. "Breathe, fix the problem, move on."

Michelle made the coffee the right way and brought it to the general, who drank as she watched the Big Board.

Michelle headed back to her cubicle, which was practically next to the command deck and very much in the general's peripheral vision. She forced herself not to crawl under her desk. She stole looks at the general's assistant, who was as cool as General Landry. The woman was young, just out of the academy maybe. She would've had to graduate best of her class to land this job, working directly with the general as adjutant. If she did two years in that spot and did well, she could write her own ticket for her next assignment. Michelle wanted to be her, to be that cool under pressure, not the kind of person who messed up something as simple as coffee.

Michelle looked at the clock: 10:35 p.m., thirty-five minutes past when she was supposed to punch out. She grabbed her backpack and headed for the exit. Nobody noticed her leaving. Her goodbye cake had been left on a side table. A few people had managed to cut out a half-dozen slices or so in the rush to mobilize for the code red. They'd left their dirty paper plates on the table. Michelle was cleaning up the mess when somebody yelled out, "I got the call sign. It was Flight 21 out of Hollow Brim, a B550 SE-11 registered to Ando Chemical Inc."

"How long ago did that bird go offline?" the general said. "Thirty-four minutes ago? I think we're safe in saying it's still in the air, then."

That got a chuckle out of everybody. Michelle needed a second to figure out what was so funny. Yes, if the plane had crashed, NATIC would have known about it by now. No plane takes thirty-four minutes to fall to earth, even if it was flying at fifty-three thousand feet.

"Let's paint a little noise into the RFD."

Landry was telling radio control to send out a general broadcast to the runaway plane's frequency. You didn't have to know where the plane was to reach it by radio.

Major Serrano ordered her logistics team to track a probable course for the runaway plane, using its LKP, or last known position.

"We have any idea who's on that plane yet?" General Landry said.

"We're getting passenger and crew lists from Hollow Brim momentarily."

Major Serrano called out to one of her techs, "How we doing on potential coordinates?"

A junior airman hurried past Michelle but turned back. "Michelle, do me a favor and get me a regular, two creams?"

She was happy to. She had to see how this one ended.

# 15

## TIM
### 7:37 p.m. PT
*In the B550, somewhere over Washington State, heading northwest toward Seattle*

Cassie was having a hard time breathing, and Tim noticed he was breathing shallowly too.

He had never seen somebody die before. He didn't think he could handle it. Last year, he'd driven his helmet into this kid's chest during a playoff game, knocked him flat. It was a tight game, and that tackle probably won it for Hartwell. Everybody was slapping Tim's helmet. They screamed so loud he couldn't hear what they were saying. They lifted him up on their shoulders and cheered. But the kid he'd hit wasn't getting up, wasn't moving. The medic brought out an oxygen setup, the kind where you squeeze a bag to force air into the person's lungs. The kid's chest rose and fell each time the medic squeezed the bag. Tim nearly stopped breathing. Had he killed the kid? He asked if he could ride in the ambulance with him, but the EMT said no. He found out later he'd fractured the kid's rib cage, and the kid's lung had collapsed. He'd heal, but for sure he'd never play football again, and maybe never breathe the same way either. Tim felt bad that night and for many nights after, too guilty to take a deep breath as he settled into bed, seeing that poor kid over and over again, laid out on the field, not breathing.

And now Cassie.

She lay on the floor. Reeva fed her oxygen through a mask. "Is your throat better or worse?"

"Same," Cassie said, but she sounded more hoarse.

Brandon took off Cassie's sneakers. Her feet were swollen, the skin about to split. "Let's roll her on her side," Brand said.

"Why?" Tim said.

"Because she's going to throw up. She'll choke on her vomit."

They rolled Cass onto her side as she threw up foam, not a lot, but pink with blood.

"Can't you text them again, Reeva?" Em said.

"I did."

"Same thing? Stand by?"

Reeva nodded.

"Stand *by*," Tim said. "How are we supposed to do that, to do nothing, to just watch Cassie choke?"

"Tim," Em said, "shh. You're freaking everybody out."

"I'm just saying what everybody else is thinking, Em."

"Then just *think* it, okay? No need to share every thought that comes to mind. Get yourself together. The last thing we need is a panic attack from you."

"Why are you being so mean to me?"

Cassie grabbed his fingers, then Em's, and made them hold hands. "Shh," she said. The oxygen mask clouded up with her breath.

# 16

## CASSIE
### 7:40 p.m. PT
*In the B550*

Cassie was past the point where she could keep pretending that somehow everything was going to be okay. When Brandon asked if her throat felt tight, she'd said it was just a little itchy. She'd lied. It felt bad, like the time she learned she was allergic to penicillin.

She had been eight years old and had taken the antibiotic for strep throat. The allergic reaction happened so slowly, over an hour that felt like forever, the fear stretched out but didn't thin. She kept telling herself she would feel better in a minute or two, then a minute or two after that. Then she was out of time.

She ran to her parents' room to wake them up. Her windpipe had narrowed. Her breath was a screechy whistle when she exhaled. Her lungs filled with what sounded like bubbling water.

Now, on the floor of the plane, she knew this reaction was going to be worse than the one seven years earlier. Cactus needles jabbed her skin, muscles, lungs. Her skin was so cold it was beginning to feel numb, but inside, deep in her gut, she was burning up. The doctor warned her that each time the body is exposed to something it doesn't like, it reacts more strongly, as if to say, *I told you I don't want this inside me.*

She used to wear a necklace that said she was allergic to penicillin, in case she passed out or was knocked out in a gymnastics fall maybe, but then the necklace broke. She never replaced it. The part of her that thrilled at taking risks had won out.

She didn't want to be that person anymore, Crazy Cass the daredevil who infuriated everyone with her insane tricks, the one who pretended she wasn't scared. She was scared all right. She was losing control of her body, of her ability to move, to breathe.

"Don't cry, Cass," Em said, crying.

She wanted Reeva's phone, to text her parents. She would have written, *Thank you for having me. I loved being here, most of the time.*

She wasn't able to ask for the phone, to form the words.

"We can't wait anymore," Em said. "We have to storm the cockpit and either get Sofia to land the plane or land it ourselves."

"Easy now, Emily," Reeva said. "Let's all take a deep breath here."

*Except I can't*, Cassie thought.

Brandon took Cassie's pulse. His fingertips were warm on her wrist, soft, and she shivered.

"Raiding the cockpit isn't possible," Reeva said. "You'll never get through the door. It's made of steel."

"Yes," Brandon said, "but the wall between the cockpit and the rest of the plane is fiberboard. I checked it. I dug the edge of my phone into the plastic coating and scratched into it. It's heavy-duty, but it's still wood. Tim's a pile driver. He'll hit the door so hard the hinges will pull away from the wall."

"Brand, you can't be serious," Tim said.

"It'll take a lot more than one run at it," Reeva said. "Tim's shoulder would break first."

"See?" Tim said.

Reeva continued, "After Sofia hears that first hit, she'll know we're trying to breach the cockpit, and she'll put us into a dive. We have to sit tight and wait for the ransom situation to play out. That's our best chance."

"Not for Cassie," Brand said. "There's a keyhole on the outside of the door."

"And the key to open it is in the cockpit," Reeva said.

"But what if you shoot the lock out, Reeva? How many shots would it take? Two, maybe three?"

"Are you kidding?" Reeva said. "One."

"Then we could get in there fast enough to overwhelm Sofia before she dumps the plane."

"You're forgetting I can't get my gun out of the safe without Tony's combination."

"But does Sofia know that?" Brandon said. "What if we *tell* her you have your gun and you're going to shoot out the lock?"

"Bluff, you mean," Jay said.

"It won't work," Reeva said.

"Why are you so set on trying to keep us from getting into the cockpit?" Em said.

Cassie would have asked the same thing if she had been able to find enough breath to speak.

"Sofia didn't get this far without knowing the protocols, that the gun gets locked up," Reeva said.

Brandon took that in and nodded. "And if we really did have the gun, we wouldn't give her a warning. We'd shoot out the lock and take her by surprise."

"Cass, don't close your eyes," Em said. "Guys, what about the ice cream machine? For a battering ram, I mean."

"Not heavy enough."

"The refrigerator," Jay said. "The one under the kitchen counter. I saw it when Reeva and I got the oxygen tank for Cassie. It's on wheels. They're held in place with spring locks. You know, like in the cafeteria? At least they had them in my school. Those things are heavy-duty metal boxes. We could get that fridge moving pretty fast with some solid weight behind it."

"Guys, say we actually manage to get in there," Tim said. "What then? Who flies the plane?"

"Tony," Em said.

"Tony's dead for sure," Tim said.

Cassie had been thinking that all along but hearing someone say it out loud suddenly made it real. In all the years she'd known Tony, she'd never once seen him upset. He was always smiling, always happy to teach Cassie about the plane. He was like that uncle who tells you you're his favorite, just don't tell anybody else.

"So who *lands* the plane?" Tim said.

"Air traffic control will help us," Em said.

"That only happens in the movies," Tim said. "Reeva's right. We wait and hope this is a ransom situation. That's our best shot at seeing our parents again. Meanwhile we make Cassie as comfortable as we can."

Emily grimaced. "How can you give up on her like this, Tim? You've known her since kindergarten."

Cassie would have hushed Em, but she couldn't get her lips to make a *Shh*. Tim was right. The best bet for everybody was to wait this out—everybody but Cassie.

"No, we live or die together," Brand said. "That's my vote. Jay?"

"I'm with you," Jay said.

"Thank you," Em said, and the way she said it, Cassie knew that if Em wasn't in love with Jay already, she was in love with him now and forever. Cassie would have smiled if she didn't feel the invisible hand around her throat clamp down a little tighter with every bit of breath she struggled to take in.

"The plane will be easier to land on the water anyway," Brandon said.

"*What* water?" Tim said. Seeing him this way, more terrified than confused, Cassie felt a dull ache in her chest. Tim had completely let down his guard, at long last. All his bravado was gone, and what was left was the real Tim, the sweet lost boy she'd come to know eleven years ago, the one who held her hand a little too tightly as they walked to kindergarten together, happy to let Cassie lead the way.

Brandon pointed out the window.

"It's beautiful," Em said. "The Pacific, Cass. It's not too far away. Hang in, okay? For me, please. You can do this."

Cassie nodded, but the air seemed filled with millions of bubbles, popping and reforming, everything turning grainy and dark.

# 17

## MICHELLE
### 10:45 p.m. ET (7:45 p.m. PT)
*Coltsville, Virginia, NATIC*

The plane had entered the restricted, radar-free flight deck in NW6 and vanished from the Big Board three quarters of an hour ago. Michelle knew that at some point it would have to reappear on the grid, either by flying out of the area's perimeter or by descending into commercial airspace. It was going to come down one way or another, either by choice or because it was running out of fuel.

There was one other possibility.

Michelle knew the general had to be thinking about it: that she would have to shoot down the plane if it seemed headed for an office tower or a hospital, or any heavily populated area. At minimum the death toll in a shoot-down would be five high school students, their chaperone, and two pilots—and maybe only one of the pilots was a bad guy.

Maybe neither was.

What if a terrorist had infiltrated the ground crew and rigged a device to leak carbon monoxide into the cockpit, and both pilots were unconscious, the plane flying blind into the restricted flight deck? What if the terrorist was still *on the plane*, had hidden in the cockpit or maybe the bathroom?

The what ifs kept coming as Michelle's laptop screen updated with information on the crew.

The captain, Tony Blake, fifty-one, had been the Ando family's personal pilot for eight years. Before that he flew for the family's corporation, Ando Chemical Inc. for a year, and before that he worked for a commercial airline. All his reports were stellar. The only bad mark on his chart was a misdemeanor for driving a car while his blood alcohol level was just over the legal limit. Blake had pled guilty and paid a sixteen-hundred-dollar fine. Because he hadn't caused any bodily harm, he was cleared to fly after attending mandatory alcohol abuse counseling sessions.

Next: Nick Sokolov, thirty-six, Tony Blake's usual copilot. He'd graduated top of his class from flight school with outstanding references. His record was perfect, not one bad mark. He too had been with the Andos for a good bit of his career—six years. A father of two, he coached soccer and had made the headlines in his community newspaper at least twice for volunteer counseling work at a local halfway house.

But he didn't report for duty the day his plane became a runaway. Why?

The FBI was looking for him. He hadn't checked out of his hotel back near Hollow Brim, Idaho, where the AWOL flight originated, but his clothes were still there, his bag half-packed, as if he'd abandoned the room in a hurry.

Then there was Sofia Palma, the last-minute replacement copilot filling in for Sokolov. She had no known family. Her parents were killed when a car bomb exploded in an open-air market in San Salvador. She had been sixteen at the time. Now at the age of twenty-three she had almost no experience flying private jets. She had gone into flight training directly from junior college and finished first in her class. Over the next three years she logged fifteen thousand hours of flying time. She was in the air more than she was on the ground. Crummy assignments too, overnight copilot jobs for cut-rate shipping companies. She must have been in a hurry to move over to private jet flight, logging so many hours so quickly. Once a pilot logged fifteen thousand hours, she was considered a strong hire.

Executive Air Staffing Inc. of Rosemont, Idaho, had snapped Palma right up. Her evaluations all said the same thing: She was professional and meticulous. Three evaluators described her as "very quiet."

So Palma had no family of her own and no connection to the Ando family. Of the three pilots, she had the least to lose.

It occurred to Michelle that all the researchers were doing the same thing she was, and almost certainly doing it better: looking into the pilots. But what about the kids?

Could one of them be in on whatever was going on up there in NW6?

Not likely. Bio workups on them wouldn't be of much interest to the general. Why, then, were Michelle's fingers tapping up Cassie Ando's Instagram?

She went through the most recently posted pictures, from a camping trip Cassie and her friends had just taken in Idaho.

Cassie and Emily Alarcón, arms over each other's shoulders after a swim in the lake. Cassie: big smile.

Cassie and Emily again, laughing as they made a mess of the s'mores they were cooking over the fire pit.

Cassie and Brandon Singh on a raft, and there it was again, that lopsided grin. Michelle saw herself in Cassie Ando, but how could that be? They were from different worlds. Michelle was a public school kid from a military family and Cassie went to a private school where the tuition was more than Michelle's dad had been making as a top-ranked air force pilot.

Michelle zoomed in on Cassie's face, and now she saw it, the thing that she and Cassie had in common. The look in Cassie's eyes, open a little too wide.

She was covering.

Was she depressed?

Why?

Had she lost something, or someone?

Even as she was the life of the party, was she lonely in a crowd?

Michelle pulled up Cassie's Facebook friends to see what they had to say about her.

She was a phenomenal athlete, captain of the gymnastics team, consistently medaled on the balance beam. Those pictures were posted by Emily, the team's manager. Hartwell Academy was for the ultra-rich, all right. What school can field a nationally competitive gymnastics team on its own? Michelle didn't know anybody who took gymnastics lessons. She was curious, stunned by all this wealth and privilege she was seeing as she clicked through Cassie's life.

Cassie had cut school last year to go to a protest. She had been arrested after she climbed a lamppost with a megaphone. The police report said she almost fell when she jumped from the lamppost to a nearby tree to escape a SWAT officer scaling the lamppost.

She was known to start food fights with boys who expressed anti-feminist views.

Major Serrano's assistant brought her an iPad. The major swiped the screen, and an update appeared on Michelle's computer monitor.

NATIC kept reaching out to the radio frequency registered to the runaway plane. Each attempt produced bounce back, which meant the plane's onboard computer was blocking all incoming transmissions.

Flight 21 had gone offline intentionally.

This was a federal crime, one that could land the perpetrator thirty years' jail time, but Michelle suspected the pilot wasn't worried about that. This update all but confirmed Michelle's suspicion that Sofia Palma had taken over the cockpit. Now came the hard part: Why?

"Well, hello there," General Landry said, looking at the giant flight-tracking screen. The red dot representing Flight 21 out of Hollow Brim had reappeared. It blinked as it headed west off the coast of northwest Washington State, out over the Pacific.

"How about we get a couple of birds up there and sneak a peek?" the general said.

Major Serrano called in the general's order. The general leaned back in her chair and stretched her arms over her head. Her eyes landed on Michelle. "I'm sorry, kiddo, one more time, what's your name?"

Michelle stammered, but she remembered this time. "O-Okolo, ma'am."

"Okolo, could you manage to bring me some coffee?" She winked at Michelle.

Boy oh boy, General Landry definitely was forgiving. More than that, she was ice when the world was on fire.

# 18

# EMILY
*7:51 p.m. PT*

*In the B550*

The refrigerator wasn't as easy to get out of the kitchenette as they had hoped. It was on wheels, but the lip of the marble countertop overhung the refrigerator by an inch and kept it pinned in place.

Jay, Brandon, and mostly Tim lifted the countertop clear of the refrigerator while Emily and Reeva unlocked the wheels and rolled the fridge out from its spot next to the sink. In the process, they destroyed the kitchen. The counter cracked apart and tore out the sink with it. The water pipes broke and sprayed until Jay turned off the valves. The drainpipe snapped too, where it came in at the floor.

Jay stepped down on the drainpipe, pushing what was left of it through the hole in the floor, which was more or less half a foot in diameter. Jay went to the floor on his stomach to look into the hole and shined his phone light through it, into the cargo hold. "Wish we could get down there, and then into the nose of the plane," he said. "There has to be a trapdoor for the mechanics to work on the cockpit controls."

"So do we try to surprise Sofia from underneath, or do we stick with the plan of ramming down the cockpit door?" Emily said.

Jay shined light on a cross section of the metal floor. "We'd need a seriously powerful circular saw to cut through that."

"Anybody got one?" Emily said. "Then let's wheel that fridge into the pass-through aisle."

They lined up behind the fridge, which they had positioned as far away as possible from the cockpit door so they could get their battering ram up to maximum speed.

Reeva watched with folded arms and a big downer of a frown. "May I offer a suggestion? You can't have more than one person push the refrigerator. You're slowing yourselves down, tripping over each other."

Everybody looked at Tim.

"Yup," he said. "Look, it's the one thing I'm good at, wrecking stuff. And anyway, you guys are right behind me, right? *Right*." He got behind the fridge like a linebacker about to drive a tackling dummy thirty yards into the end zone.

In a few seconds, they would know their fate. They'd get into the cockpit, take control of the plane, and reach out to air traffic control for help—or they would trigger a nosedive.

Suddenly, Emily wished she had more time, just enough to let Jay know how she felt, how truly grateful she was for his vote to raid the cockpit, to try to save Cassie. She looked over to him.

His focus was on the battering ram, on Tim.

Tim charged the cockpit. The others followed, ready to overwhelm Sofia when the door blew in.

Except it didn't.

The door swung open before the fridge and Tim and the rest of the crew could hit it, and then *they* were hit with a stream of white powder, a blast so strong it knocked Emily back and blinded her.

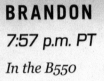

# BRANDON

## 7:57 p.m. PT

*In the B550*

In the cloud of fire extinguisher powder, there was a low-hanging circle of gold light, a pilot's view of the sunset. It disappeared when the cockpit door slammed shut. The hydraulic lock groaned and then clicked.

The blast of powder had blown Tim back into Brandon, and he'd felt himself knock over Jay.

"Tim, you're crushing me," Brandon said.

They untangled themselves and coughed up the powder. Brandon's eyes burned like someone had skimmed them with a razor blade. Reeva appeared with a liter-size bottle and trickled water into Brandon's eyes. As the fire extinguisher dust settled,

Brandon saw a body facedown in front of the door, hands tied, not moving.

"Tony?" Brandon said.

No response.

Brandon checked Tony's neck for a pulse. It was strong and fast. He went to untie Tony's hands, but Em had already loosened the binding. Sofia had used earbud wire to cuff Tony.

Why had she given him up?

Was she afraid he would regain control of the plane while she fought off the Hartwell crew? But he was handcuffed, unconscious.

Was she panicking?

The B550 made a turn so hard it knocked Brandon to the floor.

Very quickly the plane straightened out and the ride was smooth again.

Tony groaned. He put his palm to his left temple and winced. His left cheek was puffy, red. The Hartwell kids helped him to a recliner.

"What happened up there?" Emily said. She had been hit with the powder too, but not as much and not in the face.

"The weather report kept coming in bad," Tony said. "Strong winds to the east, fly west. Flight control gave us an unusually high altitude. I took the plane up, and that's when you guys checked in via the intercom. After a bit we got another order from air traffic control, take the plane even higher. I asked Sofia to confirm the altitude with ATC, because it was beyond where commercial aircraft are allowed to fly. Sofia confirmed it, or I thought she did. I wasn't wearing my headset. I reached for it to confirm the order myself with a verbal, and in the corner of my eye I saw her swinging something at my face. It might have been a full soda can in a sock. Then I don't remember anything, until her cursing woke me up."

"Cursing?" Brandon said.

"When she saw you were getting ready to break down the door," Tony said. "There's a pinhole camera hidden in the emergency light over the door in case—"

"In case somebody tries to attack the cockpit," Em said for him, shaking her head.

"The idea is that the pilot will have some lead time to radio in a mayday or try for an emergency landing," Tony said.

"Or get ready to spray the attacker with a fire extinguisher," Em said.

"We're lucky she used the powder," Tony said. "We keep two extinguishers up there. The other's foam. The powder's bad enough, but if you get the foam in your eyes, forget it, you go blind. Get it in your mouth, your lungs, you drown in your own blood. She doesn't want to kill you, clearly. You're worth a lot more to her alive." Tony fingered his temple where Sofia had hit him. His left eye was blood-shot. "I saw the report come up on the screen too. The weather report, in red text. The directions to fly northwest, to bring the plane higher and higher. They must have taken over the computer, or at least the communications interface."

"Who, though?" Em said.

Tony's eyes got wet. "I flew with him for six years," he said. "Nick was the nicest guy you could hope to work with."

"It just doesn't seem possible," Em said. "Nick loves the Andos."

"And they love him," Tony said. "Last time we flew out to Colorado, we were walking with Mr. Ando from the terminal to the limo, helping him with his bags, and his bodyguard got into it with a group of protesters. One of them broke through the police tape and rushed the boss. Nick put himself between the assailant and Mr. Ando. Mr. A said if he'd had a son, he'd want him to be like Nick."

"Protesters?" Brandon said.

"Environmental activists upset about that new chemical plant they're building on the Colorado River."

"Was Nick like that?" Brandon said. "Pro-environment, anti-industry?"

"I didn't think so," Tony said. "He'd bought a bunch of stock in Ando Chemical, he told me, but maybe he was just saying that, for cover. Do you have any water?"

Reeva handed Tony a fresh bottle.

Brandon noticed that Reeva was the only person not covered in fire extinguisher powder.

Tony chugged the water. Brandon heard a crackling sound that he thought was Tony, squeezing the plastic water bottle—but it was Cassie, gasping.

Tony blinked as if he couldn't believe what he was seeing: Cassie on the floor, on her back, her chest rising and falling too quickly. He went to her and knelt at her side. "What happened?" he said.

Brandon told him they suspected Sofia had poisoned her.

"Why?" Tony said more to himself than the others, because how could they know? How did poisoning Cassie in any way advance Sofia's goal?

Cassie had picked up a deep tan after four days hiking and swimming in the Idaho canyon lands. Brandon remembered how she looked that morning, on the slackline. She was golden. Now her face was turning blue, her lips gray. She was staring at Brandon. She tried to speak.

Brandon bent to kiss her forehead, but the kiss only seemed to agitate her more. She was trying to say something, clutching Brandon's sleeve, pleading with him. Her mouth shaped a word, but there was no breath behind it.

Brandon read her lips, and then Em said what he was thinking: "Looks like she's saying 'app,' and then something else."

Cassie nodded. "App—" Her cough cut off the rest.

Tony knelt at her side now. "What's that, sweetheart?" His tears fell on her face.

"*App*. Puh." She was becoming more upset, trying to pull Tony closer to her so she could get the word into his ear.

"Like a phone app?" Em said. "Get her phone."

Cassie shook no. Her eyeballs rolled upward and drifted to the right. She closed her eyes and gritted her teeth. "App . . . puh . . ."

She convulsed. Em and Reeva joined Brandon as he tried to comfort Cassie, but she stopped shaking soon enough. Her body twitched, a finger curl, a slight jerk of the leg, but those were just residual electrical impulses, neurons firing their last charges, Brandon knew from his biology class last year. The eyes, though. Her eyes.

Brandon's dad had talked about it, death on the operating table, the moment the person was gone and the body was just a body. People who hadn't seen it up close over and over again described the transition as the cooling of an ember or a dying spark.

They were wrong.

You couldn't fault them for remembering death that way, Pop had said. In their recollection they needed to slow things down in order to process the finality of what had happened when that person they loved just stopped *being*. They romanticized it as some gradual, gentle passage, the spirit's fading out of one place, into some other, unseen place . . . or not. But after seeing it so many times, Pop concluded that death was instantaneous. There was no fade. It was a click. You, the watcher, the one left behind, would miss it if you blinked.

Had Brandon blinked?

He was sure he'd been watching them all along, Cassie's eyes, but somehow he'd failed to see it, that moment when whatever it was that coordinated the billion trillion quadrillion atoms that had come together to be Cassie and moved her, moment by moment, through her life the past fifteen years—when that energy, that spirit vanished. What was in front of him now was a bunch of molecules that didn't know how to work together anymore.

He felt he'd betrayed Cassie in missing that moment when she took her leave. You can tell when somebody's paying attention to you. Apparently Brandon just hadn't been focused enough. Now there was no moment to romanticize or even remember.

*Wake up.*

*You're on a hijacked plane. Your best friend was likely poisoned, and now she's dead.*

*Unbelievable? Could never happen in your world?*

*Keep telling yourself that, and you'll end up dead too.*

They were still open, her eyes, but they weren't shiny. They were dry, dull.

Brandon closed Cassie's eyes. Now he could stop wondering—*had* to stop wondering—if they'd ever end up together.

# 20

## MICHELLE
### 11:02 p.m. ET (8:02 p.m. PT)
*Coltsville, Virginia, NATIC*

Michelle checked the Big Board for updates. The surveillance jets the general requested were airborne and a few hundred miles from the runaway B550.

Michelle tapped up Brandon Singh's Facebook. He didn't post a lot, mostly links to articles he found interesting, blogs and zines related to PTSD. Michelle clicked to one Brandon had written himself, an essay he'd published in the *New York Times* the year before—at fourteen years old. These kids were amazing. The essay was titled "Why I Had to Stop Dreaming."

Michelle copied excerpts to her Brandon file:

*. . . first reaction to hearing that Pop died wasn't sadness. It was fury. I wanted to kill the person who dropped that bomb on the medical aid station. That the bombing was accidental, and that the pilot, a fellow American, was suicidal with remorse we were told, did not matter to me. I wanted to kill him anyway . . .*

*. . . feeling that kind of rage was new to me. I didn't relish the sensation. It was not liberating or cathartic. I'd always found the idea of blind revenge depressing, and now I was seeking it, if only in scenarios that would come to me while I was sleeping . . .*

*. . . so for now I choose not to dream. No, I can't stop my mind from going down wormholes while I sleep, but in my waking hours I can dial everything down, the scale of my ambition. I'd hoped to be just like Pop, to become a trauma surgeon in a public hospital, a lifesaver. No more. I just don't think I have what it takes, the ability to compartmentalize loss after loss. I don't know what I want to do anymore. I don't know who to be. All I know is, I don't want to be angry.*

Michelle's second screen blipped with an invitation posted to Emily Alarcón's Facebook. A friend wanted Emily to like a page she'd set up to raise awareness about the plight of refugees detained in the tent cities growing along the Texas-Mexico border.

Emily was active in fundraising for refugee children. Her Hartwell Academy profile page—yes, the school had its own mini-Facebook—listed her as "somebody who'd love to be out in the field, doing the hands-on work with the kids, but who will probably end up in the office, deep in the trenches of nonprofit budgeting. I like being the person behind the scenes."

Michelle clicked back to the essay Brandon had written, to his confession that his first reaction to his father's death was fury. Then she clicked to his Facebook page and one of the links he'd posted about PTSD. She read that people suffering from PTSD might not even know they have it until months after the event that caused it, or sometimes even many years later.

# 21

## EMILY
### 8:04 p.m. PT
*In the B550*

Cassie Ando, dead?

Emily stopped shaking her but refused to acknowledge the possibility, the proof, the body. She looked away from Cassie to Reeva, who seemed to be emotionless, but her chest rose and fell a little too quickly.

Brandon: stony face, tear tracks.

Tony: trying not to cry, failing.

Tim: red cheeks, scrunched-up face, the way you look when you know you didn't do anything wrong but blame yourself anyway.

Jay had collapsed back into one of the recliners. He stared at the ceiling as if looking through it, toward a meteor on fire, gunning for Earth and big enough to blow up the world.

Emily heard her own voice but didn't know where the words were coming from, because how could she get it together to talk at a time like this? "She was fighting right until her last breath."

Fighting, sure enough.

Fighting for what, though?

Cassie had seemed desperate to get out one last word.

"App, puh?" Emily whispered.

"The Appaloosa horse?" Tony said. "The stuffed animal she gave me for my goddaughter. Maybe she wanted to die holding it?"

"She wasn't like that," Emily said. "Toys, *things*—she just didn't care about any of that. All she cared about was everybody else, about shaking them up, waking them up. Like, we're *alive*, you know? Let's get out there and *go* and go *crazy*. She wasn't the kind to die curled up with a stuffed animal."

She had no choice anymore but to surrender to Cassie's wish for her. Emily would pour herself into everything she cared about, with a vengeance. It wasn't enough to volunteer at the homeless shelter anymore—she would write letter after letter to Congress to get decent, humane, safe housing for the mentally ill, and she would rally others to do the same. She would treasure every opportunity to create joy, even the littlest bit of it, and while she was at it, she'd allow herself to be joyful, maybe even wildly so. She couldn't ever see herself doing cartwheels on a slackline, but maybe she'd take that flamenco dance class she'd had her eye on since she was in grade school. Okay, so maybe that was corny, and for sure she'd be the youngest person in the class, but it just looked so *fun*. Either way, from now on, Emily wasn't going to be afraid to let herself get a little out of control.

But would there be a *from now on*?

Would she get another chance to do it, to really live, the way Cassie did?

Or was she soon to follow Cassie?

She forced herself to look at the corpse, to see the face, to focus on Cassie's mouth, still partly open.

*Appuh* . . .

*Not Appaloosa horse. No way.*

Tony was looking out one of the right-side windows. Emily checked the sky. The sun was just about gone.

"She'll land it soon," Tony said.

"Crash-land it into the ocean?" Jay said.

"If crashing was the plan, she'd have hit Seattle. That was her chance to do maximum damage. We're heading south-southwest by the look of the dusk. I suspect she'll angle back toward land, probably aim for a touchdown somewhere near the coast, at one of the bigger airports where whoever is helping her can blend in with the crowd—maybe San Fran or LA. This will be over in a couple of hours. We just have to hang in until then." He sat back into the recliner, staring at Cassie. "It doesn't make sense, poisoning Cass. Hey, she was allergic to peanuts. Did you all maybe eat some candy and then touch something she ate?"

"I saw her react to peanuts once," Brandon said. "She didn't know there was peanut oil in the new salad dressing at this place we used to go to. The reaction was nothing like this. It had to be a poisoning."

"Why poison Cassie and not the rest of us?" Tim said.

"She was the only one besides Tony who might have been able to land the plane if we were successful in raiding the cockpit," Brandon said.

"But how would *Sofia* know that?" Emily said. "I *knew* Nick. I *know* him. He just wouldn't do anything to hurt Cassie—or anybody. He volunteers in a soup kitchen."

"Wake up, Em," Tim said. "He was doing that to make himself seem like a good guy, the kind who'd never be part of a hijacking."

"Easy, Tim," Emily said. "Now is not the time to lose it."

"Then when *is* a good time?" Tim said. "I'm just sick of you trusting people you don't really know." He was looking at Jay.

Jay?

No way was he in on this.

No way.

"Why are you looking at me like that?" Jay said.

"Like what?" Tim said.

"*Guys*," Emily said.

"I think we might want to consider another attempt," Reeva said.

Emily wasn't the only one who snap-turned toward Reeva.

"Attempt on the *cockpit*?" Tim said.

Reeva nodded. "We need to act fast, as in *now*."

# 22

**JAY**

*8:14 p.m. PT*

*In the B550*

"Reeva, you were dead set against attacking the cockpit not too long ago," Tim said. He looked even more panicked now, Jay thought.

"Tony's right," Reeva said. "She's angling back toward land. Look."

Jay looked out the left-side windows and saw distant lights, clumps of silver and streaks of dim gold, highways and towns along the coast—and then thickening streaks leading inland to shimmering silver, clearly a city.

"That's gotta be Portland," Tony said.

"She's going to crash the plane," Reeva said.

"How do you know?" Em said. "Why are you suddenly chang-ing your mind like this?"

"My gut."

"That's not good enough, Reeva," Brandon said. His eyes ticked from Reeva to Tony and then back to Reeva.

Jay felt a step behind. Something was happening here, between Reeva and Tony. They were staring at each other.

"If we attempt another shot at the cockpit, she'll hit us with the foam," Tim said. "No way I'm being the front guy again, taking the brunt of it. In fact, you guys can count me out. I'm with Tony: This'll be over in an hour, two tops. Let her land the plane."

"Or fly it into a baseball stadium," Reeva said. "You're not going to have to get close to the door this time, Tim. I'm going to shoot out the lock, like Brandon suggested earlier."

"Whoa, whoa, whoa, wait," Emily said. "You want the *gun* now?"

Jay watched Emily's eyes narrow the way Cassie's had whenever Reeva was around.

Had Cassie been right? Could Reeva be working with Sofia after all?

"I'll be the first through the door," Reeva said. "If Sofia so much as shows her face, I'll shoot her, center of mass, done. And then Tony can take over the controls."

"Reeva, you're the one who said Sofia would know all the pro-tocols about the gun," Emily said.

"I was wrong. I had to be. If she had known that both Tony and

I are needed to open the gun safe, she wouldn't have given us Tony. She can't know there's a gun on board."

"Wait, why *did* she put Tony out here with us, then?" Tim said.

"She was afraid he'd wake up eventually, and then he's kicking and screaming, trying to free himself while she's trying to fly the plane," Emily said.

"Then why didn't she just kill him?" Tim said. "It's because she wants him alive. She wants *all* of us alive, because this is a *ransom* thing, guys."

"Then why'd she kill Cassie?" Emily said.

"We don't know for sure that she did!"

"C'mon, Tim," Emily said. "You really think Cass died because you ate a Reese's and then touched the microwave handle, and then *she* touched the microwave handle?"

"Don't look at me that way," Tim said.

"*What* way?"

"Like I'm an idiot."

"Tim, easy," Brandon said, but Tim cut him off.

"If Sofia *did* poison Cassie somehow, some *crazy* way that none of us can figure out, then Cass's death was a mistake. She wanted her incapable of flying the plane maybe, but she wanted her alive."

"Reeva, we can't storm the cockpit," Tony said. "The spyhole camera—Sofia will see you take the gun out of the safe. She'll dump the plane into a dive and only pull out of it if you back off."

"We'll cover the camera," Reeva said.

"Then she'll *definitely* dump the plane," Tim said. "Please, you guys, just let the psycho land the plane and get her money and get *gone*. It's the only way we survive this."

Reeva pointed out a left-side window. "We're angling toward that patch of lights. The longer we debate this, the less time we have to take over the cockpit and the flight controls. We have to decide."

Getting near a city was definitely making Reeva very nervous. Was there some sort of military protocol she wasn't telling them about, like a runaway plane approaching a city gets shot down when it's ten miles out, or maybe twenty?

Reeva was right—they were running out of time and had to decide—but Tony had made a good point. Sofia would see the gun come out of the safe. Tim was right too. If they tried to block the camera, Sofia would have to assume they were going to raid the cockpit.

Everyone looked to Tony. He was staring at the cockpit door, then he looked out the window, to the growing city lights. "I still think that if she wanted to crash the plane, she would have done it by now."

"Tony, if you won't help me get the gun out of the safe, then I'll storm the cockpit myself with the battering ram," Reeva said. "Even if I can talk some of you into helping me, we'll still need two or three runs at the door, if Sofia doesn't hit us with the foam. By the time we hit that door hard enough to knock it down, Sofia will have had a half minute or more to put the plane into a free fall. With the gun, I can shoot out the lock from a distance. She won't be able to spray the foam, because the second I see that door open—whether she opens it or I shoot it open—I'll shoot her, if she doesn't come out with her hands up. With the gun, we'll breach the cockpit in seconds. That won't be enough time for her to put the plane into an unrecoverable dive. Time to choose, gang. Battering ram or gun. Either way, I'm taking a shot at that cockpit door." Reeva got behind the refrigerator and started to push it toward the door.

Jay was torn. His instinct was to help Reeva, but at the same time this nasty image was forefront in his mind: the plane in a dead-drop nosedive. In the end, Tony saved him from having to decide.

"Zero, seven, one, six," Tony said. "That's my code for the gun safe."

Tim cursed and stomped, Emily seemed relieved, and Brandon could have gone either way.

For his own part, Jay felt wobbly. The idea of having another go at the cockpit did not thrill him, but then he wasn't too happy about the alternative, hoping that Sofia was rational enough to want a ransom deal instead of a suicide crash.

The strangest reaction of all was Reeva's. She was glaring at Tony. She went to the coat closet, which opened onto the passenger aisle. Reeva opened the door so that it blocked the view of the pin-hole camera.

The plane seemed to dip a little—or was Jay imagining it?

Jay couldn't see the gun-safe keypad from where he was in the aisle, but the motion of Reeva's arm told him she tapped it four times. That had to be her code, because she asked Tony for confirmation of his. "Zero, seven, one, six?"

"Correct," Tony said, his voice shaky.

Tim paced and pulled at his hair.

Brandon was motionless next to Tony.

Jay felt Emily grab his hand for the second time as Reeva keyed in Tony's code.

The safe door didn't open.

# 23

# MICHELLE
*11:23 p.m. ET (8:23 p.m. PT)*
*Coltsville, Virginia, NATIC*

The stuff Michelle had compiled on Cassie, Brandon, and Emily was interesting, but none of it seemed useful to the investigation. She was about to look into Tim and especially Jay, the newcomer to the group, when she remembered what Major Serrano had told her not too long ago, that information was important but just as important was knowing how to prioritize it. Yes, everybody on the plane was a potential suspect, but who was more likely to be a hijacker: a kid who had a huge future to look forward to, or an adult with an ax to grind? That's what had made Michelle shift gears to the chaperone, Reeva Powell, and she'd struck gold. She quickly scanned what she'd found so far:

A simple Google search revealed that Reeva was suing the government, specifically Medicaid. Her mother's Parkinson's required round-the-clock care, Reeva stated in her lawsuit, and Medicaid sent health-care aides to the apartment for only eight hours a day. Reeva, working full time, cared for her mom during the nights and paid for private nursing assistance to cover the hours she couldn't be there.

But now Reeva was broke. Her credit report said she was struggling to keep up with the interest-only payments on a hundred and fifty thousand dollars she owed a sketchy financial services company, basically a loan shark with a website.

Reeva needed help. When she had to work late, she'd been forced to leave her mom alone, and Mrs. Powell fell and hit her head. She was in intensive care for five weeks. Some of the doctors in the hospital didn't accept Medicaid, and the bills from that one fall were part of the reason Reeva had to take out the high-interest loan.

Reeva Powell was desperate for cash.

Michelle checked the Big Board for any news. The Pacific time zone clock said 8:24 p.m.

## 24

**TIM**

*8:24 p.m. PT*

*In the B550*

Tim didn't like the look on Reeva's face as she stared at the door of the gun safe. She had lost her trademark calm. "Let's try it one last time, Tony. Zero, seven, one, six is your code. You're *sure*?"

"It's my birthday, July sixteenth."

Reeva tried again.

Nope.

"Guys, is the plane dipping?" Tim said, staggering a bit. Or was he just imagining it was dipping, more like *dropping*?

Tony stepped toward the safe. "Here, Reeva, let me—"

"Stay right there," Reeva said.

"Reeva," Tony said, "we're all on the same side here."

Reeva glared at him. Something was way wrong.

"Try putting in my code first, then," Tony said.

"It doesn't matter which goes first," Reeva said.

"Then you must have put yours in wrong," Tony said.

Reeva turned back to the keypad.

Tony whipped his nearly full water bottle at her head. The bottle was plastic but the cap was on tight. It probably weighed three times what a baseball did and hit Reeva in the face. She went down, her hands over her left eye.

Tony rushed the safe and tapped the keypad.

The safe door swung open.

Tony reached in with both hands. One hand came back out with the gun and the other with the ammunition clip.

Wait, what was Tim supposed to do now? Clearly Reeva and Tony were *not* on the same team. What team was Tim supposed to be on? Which team had the best chance of winning, or at least surviving?

From the floor, Reeva kicked Tony's knee. His leg buckled, and as he went down, she kidney-punched him. He hit the floor and rolled away just clear of her so she couldn't grab the gun. He pushed the clip into the gun and pointed it at her. From his knees he said, "Reeva, freeze. I swear I'll do it."

But Reeva kept coming at him.

Tony pulled the trigger.

Tim winced, anticipating the sound of the shot.

It didn't come.

Reeva kicked the gun from Tony's hand. It landed practically at Tim's feet. As much as he'd wanted to try it out back at the campsite, he didn't even want to touch it now. So then why was he bending down to pick it up, reaching for it, the gun an inch from his hand?

Reeva snatched it and clicked something on the side of the gun—the safety. She pointed it at Tony. "It'll fire this time," she said.

Tony put up his hands.

"Back up," Reeva said. He did, on his knees. Reeva swung the gun toward Tim.

"Whoa," Tim said. "*Whoa!* Why me?"

"Because you're standing too close to me. Back up. Everybody stay absolutely still until I give you direction to move."

"Cassie was right," Emily said, though she stayed absolutely still, Tim noticed. "You were in on this all along."

Reeva ignored her. "Tony, get onto the floor, facedown. Put your hands behind your back. Brandon, Jay, I need you to tie him up, hands very, *very* tight. Use Brandon's belt."

"Don't do it, Brand," Emily said.

"Brandon, cuff Tony, or I will have to shoot him. He's the one. He's working with Sofia."

"That's not possible," Tim said.

"And why not?" Reeva said.

"Because . . ." Tim couldn't think of anything other than he didn't *want* Tony to be in on this. If Tony was rotten, then where did that leave the Hartwell crew in terms of their chances of making it off the plane alive?

"I was thinking the same thing about you, Reeva," Tony said. "And even if you're not in on this deal, you're going to get us killed, trying to get into that cockpit."

"Tony, stop talking, or I really will have to shoot you." Reeva turned to the others. "Gang, *think*. Tim, when the cockpit door opened and the fire extinguisher blasted you, did you actually *see* Sofia? Because I didn't."

She was right. The person holding the extinguisher had been a silhouette with the sunset coming into the cockpit. It *could* have been Tony. But . . .

"But then how did he end up on the floor?" Tim said.

"He blinded everybody and filled the hallway with a cloud of powder," Reeva said. "He tossed the extinguisher back into the cockpit and dropped to the floor. Then he let the door slam behind him. Sofia stayed by the flight controls to drop the plane, in case the cockpit breach was successful."

Everything Reeva was saying made sense, and on top of that she *looked* sensible in her nice clean suit while the rest of them were a wild mess with all the powder on their clothes, in their hair. Wait, Reeva was the only person on the plane who hadn't been hit with the powder . . .

It was happening too fast. Tim was woozy with too many thoughts swirling in his brain, or maybe because the plane was turning again, though he couldn't be sure of even that much. Maybe the turning, dipping—the whole hijacking—was in his mind. "Please let this be a bad dream," he heard himself whisper.

Reeva looked at him with disgust. "Tim, wake up. Brandon, Emily, Jay, *be logical.*"

"But if Tony really was the one who sprayed us, how did he handcuff himself with the earbud wire?" Tim said. "It was like three seconds from the time the fire extinguisher blasted us, and then Tony was on the floor, hands tied behind his back."

"They weren't," Reeva said, "not tightly anyway. I thought that was strange, that Sofia hadn't done a better job restraining him. The wire was loose enough for Tony to get his hands in there, fast. It was an act. Brandon, Jay, for the last time, cuff him."

"I'm not resisting," Tony said, "but we have to back away from the cockpit door." And he really didn't seem to be resisting Brandon and Jay as they clamped their hands on his wrists. They didn't seem eager to cuff him, but they didn't look too sure about letting go of him either. Tony nodded toward the cockpit. "She sees what's going on here. She sees the gun. We're beginning to lose altitude. Can't you feel it?"

Tim followed Tony's eyes to the cockpit. The coatroom door had swung shut in the scuffle, and Tim could see the emergency light over the cockpit entrance, where the pinhole camera was.

"Guys, everybody back up," Tim said. "We have to show Sofia we're not going to rush the cockpit with the gun. Seriously, Tony's right, the plane keeps dipping."

"It's been flying like this the whole time," Reeva said, "side to side, up and down. You're only noticing it now because he's calling your attention to it. It'll level off."

"Just the same," Tony said, "it can't hurt to retreat a little, right?"

"Please, Reeva," Tim said. "Backing up can't hurt."

"You all first," Reeva said.

Tim backed up so fast he tripped into one of the recliners.

"See," Tony said, "it's leveling off."

"It's *been* leveling off," Reeva said. "Brandon, tell everybody how tight that earbud wire was around Tony's wrists before you and Emily took it off. Or how tight it *wasn't*, rather."

"Em loosened it before I got to it," Brandon said.

"No, I didn't," Em said.

"Was it loose or *not*?" Tim said. "Brand?"

"Loose enough for him to get his hands into?" Brand seemed to have to think about it. "I can't say for sure. He could have been trying to wriggle his way out of the wire, and with his head all messed up after Sofia hit him, in his confusion, groggy, he didn't remember trying to free himself."

"The last thing I remember was getting whacked in the side of the head," Tony said, "and then I was facedown on the floor, and you and Emily were setting me free."

Reeva looked over her shoulder, toward the cockpit.

# 25

# EMILY

## 8:28 p.m. PT

*In the B550*

Reeva turned back to Tony. She aimed the gun at his head. "Tell Sofia this ends now. She lands the plane, or I kill you."

"That won't work," Brandon said. "You won't rush the cockpit with Tony dead, because who lands the plane, then? She knows Cassie's dead by now."

"Reeva, he's right," Jay said. "We're back to letting Sofia land the plane where she wants and hoping this is a ransom situation."

"It can't be, at this point," Reeva said. "Not after Tony came out of the cockpit and said he doesn't want us going in there."

"I didn't say I didn't want you going in there. I said Sofia will dump the plane if you do. And then when you wanted the gun, I knew you were the accomplice. You're new to the family, Reeva. You've been pushing all along to sit tight, the kids said. But you didn't think they would rush the cockpit. You thought they'd listen to you and wait. Then I get thrown out here and you panic, because this wasn't part of the plan, right?"

"He's right," Tim said. "He's *right*."

"Hang on," Emily said. "If Reeva's with Sofia, then why would she want to rush the cockpit?"

"Exactly," Reeva said.

"Then why are you pointing the gun at us?" Tony said.

"I'm pointing it at *you*," Reeva said.

"You were pointing it at *me* before," Tim said.

"If she's with Sofia, then she isn't going to *raid* the cockpit," Tony said. "She'll *run* to it, and Sofia will let her in. Then they'll lock the door, the both of them in there with the gun."

"So?" Reeva said. "If your plan is to wait this out, why would you care if I'm in there with Sofia?"

"Because with everybody's emotions running high, I can see the kids panicking and taking another shot at breaching the cockpit. You'll have to shoot them."

"Not *me*," Tim said. "I'm not going near that cockpit."

"I'm not losing another one of my passengers," Tony said, looking at Emily.

"Then why wouldn't I just shoot you all now?" Reeva said.

"Because a plane full of dead hostages doesn't do you any good," Tony said. "The other thing is, as much as I can't figure out why you're acting the way you are, waving around the gun, I can't be a hundred percent sure you *are* with Sofia." He nodded at the gun. "Why'd you even bother to lock it up in the first place?"

"You wanted it locked up as much as I did," Reeva said. "You played it off nonchalantly, 'It's a family flight, Reeva,' but you knew that if I had the gun, I'd be able to storm the cockpit."

"We agree on one thing," Tony said. "I definitely do not want you to have that gun."

"This doesn't have to be an either-or situation," Emily said. "Tony, Reeva, you suspect each other, but say you both really are on the same side."

"Which side?" Tim said. "Good or *bad*?"

"Tony, you're saying this is a ransom scenario, and we're better off letting Sofia land the plane. Reeva, you told us before that we had to be logical. Whether or not Tony ends up being right, his thinking is logical. Up until a little while ago, you were saying the same thing: We should wait this out. What's your reason for going into attack mode?"

"I would have gotten word from the folks on the ground that there has been a ransom request," Reeva said. She drew her phone and tossed it to Emily. "Check the text stream. See how I've been giving updates, including that Cassie is dead? Check the responses.

They keep saying stand by, that they haven't heard from the hijackers."

Emily scanned the text stream. Reeva was telling the truth.

"That text stream is between you and Sofia," Tony said. "If it isn't, then why don't you just call your supposed contact on the ground and let us hear his voice."

"It would be a *her*, first of all—"

"Right, as in Sofia."

"Tony, give her a chance," Emily said.

"Up here, using direct satellite connection, the system doesn't support audio or video," Reeva said. "NASA doesn't allow it."

"How convenient," Tony said.

"NASA is using the same satellites I am, for their transmissions, and they need to keep the traffic as clear as possible," Reeva explained more to the Hartwell crew than Tony, plainly trying to win them over to her side. "Emergency texts are permissible, but the system isn't set up to carry data packages larger than that."

"Say we believe you," Tony said. "Just because there's no ransom request yet doesn't mean there won't be."

"When?" Reeva said. "When we're on the ground? What's keeping us on the plane once we land and the threat of a crash is over?"

"There has to be a ground team component to this," Tony said. "Maybe they have the plane targeted with sniper rifles or a rocket-propelled grenade. All the hijackers have to say is that there's a bomb on the plane. It doesn't matter if there is or not. The hostage negotiators will err on the side of caution and proceed as if the bomb threat is real."

"And then what?" Reeva said. "Say bags of ransom cash are delivered to the plane. Or the bad guys set up some sort of electronic money transfer system, untraceable, if such a thing exists. How does Sofia get away?"

"I don't think she's planning to, and I don't think this is a money thing," Tony said. "I'm betting the ransom is a person, some kind of prisoner release, maybe a terrorist. But let's just go with what Emily said. Neither one of us is in on the hijacking. Reeva, you absolutely cannot try to breach that cockpit. It doesn't take *a few seconds* to put the plane into a dive, like you suggested before. It takes a split second. If she knows you're getting into the cockpit—and she will, the instant you step toward that camera with the gun in your hand—she'll push the steering mechanism all the way forward and cut the engines. By the time I get in there, no way will I be able to pull us out of that dive."

"I don't believe you," Reeva said. "Even if she *could* cut the engines midflight, which seems highly unlikely, at this speed the plane would coast long enough for you to get the engines back online and level out the plane. It'll take me three seconds to get into that cockpit."

Emily imagined what that would be like, the engines dead all of a sudden, no whirring vibration, just this terribly eerie quiet for a few seconds, before the plane started to dip.

"Reeva, I'm begging you," Tony said. "This is suicide."

But Reeva was done with the debate. She turned to the cockpit door.

"Reeva, wait!" Tim said.

"Gang, stop her," Tony said.

And they did, or tried to anyway. Tim put himself in front of Reeva the way he did in his football games, crouched and ready to hit hard, like, *No way you're getting past me.* Brandon and Jay were rushing to Tim's side, and before Emily knew it, she found herself joining the others in tackling Reeva. Somebody's knee hit Emily's cheek, and somebody else stepped on her hand. For a second she was pinning Reeva, and then Reeva was on top of her. It was a melee, everyone fighting for the gun.

Tim drove Reeva into the wall that separated the coat closet from the passenger cabin so hard he broke it. Emily heard the air whoosh from Reeva's lungs. She croaked out something between a gasp and a moan.

Tim drove her into the wall again, and now Emily heard a crunching sound, not the wall this time. The sound came from inside Reeva. Reeva's head whiplashed into the wall and then off it. Her head swung so far forward, her face almost hit her chest.

"Tim, stop!" Emily said.

"She's gonna get us killed!"

Brandon and Jay struggled to keep Tim from driving into Reeva a third time. They hung on to his arms, unable to slow him down.

Blood dripped from Reeva's mouth. Her eyes rolled back. Every time Reeva breathed, Emily heard the sound of air escaping from a tire.

"This might be game over," Tony said. "If Sofia doesn't drop the plane now, we know for sure this is a ransom situation." He had the gun. He stood in front of the camera to show Sofia he was putting it in his waistband. He backed away from the camera and the cockpit door.

# 26

## MICHELLE
### 11:33 p.m. ET (8:33 p.m. PT)
*Coltsville, Virginia, NATIC*

Michelle studied the video the FBI uploaded to the NATIC server. They had picked up the usual copilot, Nick Sokolov, at his hotel. He said he was coming in from an urgent care center after he couldn't stop throwing up. The doctor had given him some medication, and it was working great. He was feeling a hundred percent now, ready to grab the next plane home to New York.

Sokolov did look in excellent health. He also looked like he was trying not to sweat. The agents had interviewed him in one of the hotel's empty conference rooms.

Agent Choi: *But how do you know Sofia Palma?*

Sokolov: *I don't. I told you that. You keep trying to get me to say I know her. At this point I really do need a lawyer.*

Choi: *Nick, we're getting you one, but those kids up there in the plane, they're running out of time.*

Sokolov: *I know, and that's the only reason I'm talking to you right now. I want to help if I can. Cassie and the Andos, they're family to me.*

Michelle stopped the video and zoomed in on his face. He did look genuinely concerned. Michelle hit rewind and then play.

Choi: *Walk me through it again, from dinner last night.*

Sokolov: *Tony and I went to the hotel dining room. I got the shrimp. It looked really good, fresh, but now that I think about it, that first bite maybe tasted a little bit off. And the other thing, it was the special. I worked in restaurants when I was a kid. The special is usually what they couldn't sell the night before, so they cut the price to get rid of it before it rots. You throw a new sauce on it, it looks great, bingo, the food sells out fast, except maybe it already went bad. But like I said, it looked and smelled great, so I dove in. An hour later I was on my knees in front of the toilet bowl. I called Tony. He told me to sleep in tomorrow—today, and he'd call the staffing agency for a replacement.*

Michelle rewound and re-watched. Something wasn't right there, where Sokolov was talking about dinner. He seemed to be telling the truth, but . . .

But what?

She checked Sokolov's Facebook page. He had 1,121 friends, and none of them crossed with any names on the NSA's terror watch list.

Sofia Palma was a total ghost on social media. Michelle clicked to a link from an email interview one of the FBI agents did with somebody at Executive Air Staffing Inc. Nick Sokolov from Ando Chemical called in a request for Sofia specifically. The Executive manager suggested Palma was too green to copilot the B550. She'd only flown simulations on the computer. Executive had plenty of pilots with a lot more B550 experience who would be better for the job, but Sokolov was insistent that they send over Sofia Palma.

Michelle clicked to the FBI-Sokolov interview again.

Agent Choi: *Then if you don't know Sofia Palma, just help me understand why you requested her specifically to replace you.*

Sokolov: *Again, I didn't. Tony said he was going to call to get the sub.*

Choi: *And he did, but he just said send over your best B550 pilot. The manager at Executive Air said you called a while later to request Palma by name.*

Sokolov: *No way. Not me.*

Choi: *The phone ID came up with your name and number.*

Sokolov: *I gave you my phone. You checked my call history. You know I didn't make that call.*

Choi: *Not from the phone you gave us anyway.*

Sokolov: *Then it was from a burner phone, right, with no ID?*

Choi: *Great guess, Nick.* Really *great guess.*

Sokolov: *It's only logical. Somebody bought a burner phone and pretended to be me.*

Choi: *You have this all figured out, don't you?*

*Maybe,* Michelle thought. But the person trying to frame Nick, if he was in fact being framed, would not buy a burner phone in Nick's name, because what terrorist would be that careless? Nick was top of his class in flight school, way past smart. In order for the frame job to be convincing, the phone couldn't have a caller ID that connected it to Sokolov. But that didn't mean that Nick *didn't* make the call.

The NSA was checking with Executive Air to see if they recorded their calls, in the hope they could check for a voice match with Nick Sokolov, but getting that together would take at least until tomorrow morning, and Michelle had a feeling this was going to be over way before that.

She clicked back to Reeva Powell's Facebook page. Powell was not at all active. Last time she had been on was two years ago. Five friends, all clean. Profile picture was Reeva on the boardwalk with an older woman in a wheelchair. Reeva was a relatively new hire at Ando Chemical, but Mr. Ando himself thought so highly of her he detailed her to look after his only child.

Michelle tapped her mouse to the communal update screen. Nothing. The last words that had come in from Reeva Powell were *Cassie Ando is dead.*

Michelle felt she had lost a sister when the text came in—a sister she'd never gotten to know. Even now, half an hour later, she was still clamping her teeth to keep them from chattering—something she learned to do in the days after her father had died so unexpectedly.

The Big Board flashed with an update. The blinking red dot that represented the runaway plane was heading south, about fifty miles off the coast of Northern California. Three hundred fifty miles to the east and closing in fast on the red dot were two blinking blue dots that originated from Colorado Springs, Schriever Air Force Base, not far from the academy Michelle hoped she'd be attending a year from now. Those F-22 Raptors were flying Mach 2, which meant they would be on top of the B550 in less than fifteen minutes.

In a quarter of an hour, Michelle Okolo would very likely get a peek into what was happening inside that Barracuda.

# 27

## BRANDON
### 8:48 p.m. PT
*In the B550*

Brandon, a runner, couldn't remember feeling so completely exhausted. He was doing chest compressions, pounding away on Reeva's heart. Tony breathed into Reeva's mouth by way of a pocket mask.

They had been going at it for a quarter of an hour. Jay swapped out with Brandon every two minutes, because doing compressions for that long was exhausting, not to mention surreal.

A couple of Reeva's ribs must have cracked when Tim hit her, but now, after being hammered on for fifteen minutes, they were broken.

Brandon finished a round of thirty compressions, and Tony breathed into her twice.

Tim sat on the floor, away from the rest of them. He was mumbling to himself, shaking his head, and Em was trying to console him. Brandon couldn't hear what she was saying, but whatever the words, they weren't connecting with Tim.

After two minutes of compressions, Jay jumped in to replace Brandon, who could barely catch his breath. Jay was as sweaty and worn out as Brandon.

Brandon's dad had warned him that you'd never spend more energy than you did when doing CPR. While that assessment was true in regard to the toll it took on you physically, Brandon realized now that Pop meant it wore you out emotionally, spiritually. Trying and failing to bring a person back to life was devastating. Brandon had never felt so completely powerless. Reeva was dead for sure, her eyes open but seeing nothing.

They had hooked up the shock pads to Reeva's chest, one near her right collarbone, the other on the left side of her mashed rib cage. The defibrillator's automated voice sounded oddly cheerful. *"Stop compressions. Analyzing patient. Analyzing patient. No shock advised. Continue CPR."*

The cheeriness in the machine's voice infuriated Brandon. If he'd had the energy, he would have screamed. The contrast between the machine's peppiness and Reeva's lifelessness was freaky.

"Mrs. Ando must know about Cass by now," Tim said. "You think she'll ever be able to recover? Life without Cassie? And who's gonna take care of Reeva's mom?"

"Shh," Em said. "Don't talk. Just breathe."

"Why?" Tim said. "I mean, really, does it matter at this point whether or not we keep breathing?"

Tony sat back against the wall, and then Brandon, and then Jay, too wasted to continue the CPR.

The plane was too quiet.

Too still.

Brandon felt himself fading, falling asleep. He had to keep moving, before he passed out.

Action.

They needed to take action.

"We have to make another attempt on the cockpit," Brandon said.

"It's a death wish, Brandon," Tony said.

"You already said that, and maybe you're right. But here's the thing I can't figure out: Sofia hasn't made any contact with us. That makes no sense. If we really were going to land someplace and then be set free after a few hours, she should have told us by now. Especially after we tried to raid the cockpit. Not talking to us only gets us more agitated. I don't think she has any intention of landing this plane."

"The best argument that she does is that we're still airborne," Tony said.

"Then we're back to a vote," Brandon said.

"This again," Tim said.

"Em?" Brandon said. They had been friends since pre-K.

Emily nodded.

Tim spun away from her and punched the wall. "You guys are insane," he said. "Tony's the pilot. He's trained in this stuff, what to do in a hijacking. Just, please you guys, *listen* to him. Just let it *land*, before somebody else dies."

"Tim, be rational," Brandon started to say.

Tim cut him off. "Rational? Are you kidding me? Reeva was supposedly the most rational one here, and look at her now. Yeah, no, if that's rational, I don't want any part of it."

Brandon nodded to Jay. "Sorry, man, it all comes down to you."

# 28

## JAY
### 8:51 p.m. PT
*In the B550*

Jay stared at his left hand. His fingers were swollen—not from the pile-on that killed Reeva, but from doing CPR on her. He held them up to one of the overhead lights to get a better look at the damage.

"Jay, wake up," Tim said. "Did you hear Brandon? What's your vote? Raid or wait it out?"

"I need a minute," Jay said.

"Dude, where you going?" Tim said.

"To get some ice. My hand is messed up."

"Is he serious?" Tim said.

Jay went into the kitchenette and filled a Ziploc with soda machine ice and held it with his beat-up hand. The others continued debating, and then that turned into an argument between Tim and Emily. Jay moved farther back in the plane to think.

The logical thing would be to side with Tony. As much as Jay didn't want to admit it, Tim made a lot of sense when he said that Tony was the only one trained to deal with a situation like this.

But Brandon was right too. It was weird that Sofia wasn't talking to them. Then again, if she had said something like, *Chill out, you guys are going home as soon as the ransom is paid*, why should they believe her? She'd tell them the same thing if she was going to crash the plane.

He was pretty sure of it now: He was never going to see his mom again.

She was missing a tooth, the first molar on the right side. He kept telling her to get it fixed, even tried to give her money for it for her birthday, six hundred dollars he'd taken out of the college fund he was building by delivering those store circulars before school. She put the money back into his account.

She'd want him to fight, to never give up. Emily's mom had to feel the same way, and Brandon's and Tim's. They were all in the same situation, the four survivors from Hartwell. Yes, he'd only been to the school once, for orientation, but like it or not, he was one of them now, no better or worse, a hostage.

He stared at Cassie. They'd wrapped her in blankets with the oxygen tank next to her, on its side. Something drew him to it, the way a dream makes you wonder how it applies to your real life. This tank was empty, but the second one in the kitchen was still full. If they survived a crash, the oxygen would come in handy. It was supposed to calm you down. Jay could have used some supplemental oxygen right about then.

He went back to the kitchenette for a second bag of ice, for Tony this time. The poor guy kept rubbing his temple where Sofia had hit him. It wasn't actually the temple, though. It was more above his right eye, the redness. Jay wondered if Tony's vision had been compromised. If he actually did get a chance to land the plane, would he be able to?

Wait.

Why was Tony rubbing the right side of his head now? He'd been rubbing the left side before, hadn't he? And that's where the redness had been too, when they found him on the floor after the attack with the fire extinguisher—on the left side. And now that Jay thought about it, Tony had given two different stories about waking up after Sofia knocked him out. At first he'd said he'd come to when she started cursing, in the cockpit, but then he said he'd woken up later, when Brandon and Emily were untying his hands.

# 29

## EMILY
### 8:54 p.m. PT
*In the B550*

Emily waited for Tim to yell himself out. Arguing with him was useless. At this point he wasn't hearing anything she was saying. Even when she agreed with him that yes, this was the worst situation they had ever been in, he kept talking right over her. Finally he slumped into one of the recliners.

The momentary quiet was such a relief, a chance to slow everything down and take stock. If only they could get one of their phones to push out a text to the people on the ground with an update about Reeva. Maybe her death changed the math here. Maybe they did need to make another run at the cockpit. The people on the ground would be able to advise her. Then she remembered, they had a working phone now, Reeva's iPhone.

But the phone wasn't in her pocket.

Had she lost it in the scuffle, when they tried to restrain Reeva?

She looked around the floor, under the seats, but the phone was gone.

"Brand, do you have Reeva's phone?"

"I have it," Tony said. He was checking the text stream. "They keep telling her to stand by, stand by, stand by. I don't know why she didn't just listen to them."

"So now you're saying she wasn't in on the hijacking?" Brandon said.

"I don't think we can be sure one way or the other," Tony said, "but I do know that either way she had to be stopped from getting into the cockpit."

Emily eyed the phone in Tony's hand. It was metallic green.

Green like a Granny Smith apple.

"Oh no," she said. "Tony, you— No."

"Em?" Brandon said.

"*Apple*," Emily said. "That's what Cassie was trying to say. Not Appaloosa. Apple. The slices of Granny Smith apple Tony gave her when we went to visit him in the cockpit to give him the Appaloosa horse. That's why nobody else got sick. Cass was the only one who ate the apple. It was her favorite snack." She turned to Tony, her face on fire with the blood rushing into it. "After hanging around the family all these years, you knew that. You set her up, Tony. You poisoned her. You poisoned Cassie. Why? *Why?*"

He didn't deny the allegation. He didn't answer her question either. It all made sense now, what they had considered earlier: Cassie was the only one who could land the plane in the event the Hartwell crew was able to get into the cockpit and overpower Sofia—and Tony. He had thought of every last contingency.

Tony didn't look smug. No mustache-twirling villain here, Emily thought. He looked exhausted and, more than that, just really sad, almost like he didn't want to be doing this. But whatever remorse he felt, it didn't stop him from pointing the gun at Emily. "My friend, if you take one more step toward me, you'll go the way of Reeva. That much I promise you. I didn't want her to die."

"Reeva or Cass?" Emily said.

"Both. I wanted Cassie to fall asleep. I honestly didn't know she was allergic to it, the drug."

"*Honestly?*" Emily said.

"It was an over-the-counter sleep aid. I wanted *all* of you to take it. I tried to get you to pass around those apple slices, Emily. If you had, by the time you all woke up, this thing would be over and done, and other than being a little groggy, you'd be no worse for wear."

"Except for Cassie," Brandon said.

Tony aimed at Brandon. "Stop, Brandon. Stay there, I'm begging you. I never wanted it to get to this point." Tony's eyes were wet. He wiped them. He slammed Reeva's phone facedown onto the hardwood arm of one of the seats. He threw it to Emily. "Does it work?"

The screen was cracked. The phone was dead. "No."

"Good. Now you have one less option, one less thing to worry about. So here's how things are going to go, no debate. Do as I say, and you'll live."

"Why should we believe you?" Emily said.

"For starters? Because you have no choice."

"Then go ahead and shoot us," Emily said. "Seriously, go ahead. Except you can't. Once we're dead, there's no reason not to shoot down the plane."

"You're right, but I can kill some of you," Tony said. "As long as I have one of you left, they'll let the plane land. You don't have to fight here, Emily. None of you do. Just let it happen. We're all gonna sit here together and let Sofia do her thing."

"But what is that?" Emily said. "The thing that Sofia's going to do. Can't you just tell us that much? It's not knowing that makes us feel like we have to do something, anything to try to save ourselves."

"Will you sit tight, then?" Tony said. "If I tell you how this is going to play out, then you'll take your seats and know that all of this will be over in two hours? Because it will. *Less* than two hours, and you're free."

"How can we trust you after you've been lying to us the whole time?" Tim said. He looked ready to kill Tony, if only Tony hadn't swung his arm to point the gun at him now.

"Because we're still in the air," Tony said. "We dropped off the radar for a while, to get a head start on them."

"Who?" Em said.

"The air force?" Brandon said.

Tony nodded. "We're back on the air traffic control screens for sure, for a while now. If they saw this plane anywhere near a city, they'd have turned it into a fireball, no matter how much you and your families are worth. We planned our route to show the folks on the ground, the ones who can call in the kill order, that we have no intention of taking out anything with a suicide strike. The whole time we've been in the air, the plane's trajectory has been over water and low-to-no-population areas. That's the way it's going to stay too. Look out the left windows. See those patches of city lights here and there? We're staying away from them, right? Forty miles off the coast. We'll keep this far out, all the way down the coast, till we get to just north of Los Angeles. From there we're heading inland, due east over the Los Padres National Forest the whole way, nothing on the ground beneath us but pinewood."

"We're landing in the *forest*?" Tim said.

"On a lake in the forest, at the eastern edge of it," Tony said. "Pyramid Lake."

"How are you going to land on a lake at night?" Emily said.

"This plane can land in pitch-black, no runway lights," Tony said. "The dark is no problem. The camera that feeds into the flight control computer has night vision. Even without Sofia or me, the autopilot software would be able to land the plane. That lake is as smooth as a runway. Once the plane touches the water, the flotation system activates, and half an hour after that your only worry will be that each of you is going to write the same 'How I Spent My Summer Vacation' essay."

"Why there, though, Tony?" Emily said. "Why Pyramid Lake?"

"It's secluded with lots of pine tree cover for the rest of our team. That means no SWAT crew will dare raid the plane for fear one of our snipers will pick them off—and they will if they have to."

"What did you mean when you said, 'without you or Sofia'?" Emily said. "You said the plane could land on its own. Why would the plane suddenly be without you two?"

"In the extremely unlikely event we were to be killed by five very angry teenagers," Tony said.

"Four now," Emily said. The fact that Cassie was gone made all this so much worse. Cassie would have figured out a way to stop this, or she would have died trying. She never even got that much, the chance to try to end this one way or another.

She wondered what Cassie would say to her right now, if she was here. *Don't go down that road, Em. Don't fall into self-pity. You can figure this out. There's always a way. Force yourself to be calm,* *and* think.

Think about the fact there are four of you and only two of them. Tony couldn't shoot all four of them at once. Even if just one of the Hartwell crew survived, maybe a crash could be prevented and lives on the ground saved.

*If* the plane was going to crash.

Tony's no-crash scenario made sense, Emily had to admit. The remote location for the landing site and the excellent cover the trees would provide for the snipers, whoever they were—it all added up. If you were a terrorist organization looking to raise millions or demand the release of one of your confederates, this was an excellent way to do it.

But why had Tony tipped his hand like that, telling them the plane could land without him or a pilot?

Brandon must have been thinking the same thing. He said, "Let us talk with Sofia. Even by the intercom, just to let her know we're going to comply."

"No," Tony said. "You needed to know how this was going down. I told you. That's it. You're not getting anywhere near that cockpit. She and I agreed that if there's a breach, she ditches the plane."

"Then one last question," Emily said. "How are you going to let the people on the ground know we're all right, the four of us who are left? Even if Sofia gets on the cockpit radio and tells them we're okay, aren't they going to want proof? Won't they need to hear our voices?"

"They won't need audio when they have a visual." Tony pointed out a right-side window.

An air force fighter jet flew parallel with the Andos' plane, maybe fifty feet off the right wing.

"Wave, kids," Tony said, aiming the gun at them so the fighter pilot could see it. "Wave and smile. Go on now, right up to the windows, one window apiece."

"And then what happens, Tony?" Emily said. "After we land on the lake, assuming we survive that. What happens next?"

"All you need to know is that your part in this thing will be over. You'll be in a nice warm hotel less than an hour after we land."

"Why, though?" Emily said.

"Do you mean, why *you*?" Tony said.

"No, Tony, why *you*? Why are you doing this? For who?"

"You wouldn't understand," he said.

"What did Mr. Ando ever do to deserve this?" Emily said.

"Mr. Ando did nothing. Absolutely nothing at all." Tony stepped toward Emily and put the nose of the gun to her temple. She could see Tim and Brandon fighting the urge to rush Tony.

"Guys, don't," she said. "Don't move, and he won't shoot."

"Listen to her, boys," Tony said. "We don't want to make any stupid mistakes here, right? Not when we're so close to getting through this thing." He looked to the pilot of the fighter jet and gestured with a wave that the air force had seen enough, and now it was time for the fighter jet to get lost.

And it did, with a fast roll downward. The coast was clear now, nothing but moonlight and a few of the brighter stars.

"Good," Tony said, and then there was a metallic flash coming from behind him, from the back of the plane. Emily ducked, but the whirling piece of metal wasn't meant for her.

An oxygen tank spinning end over end hit the Ando family's longtime pilot in the right temple, and Tony Blake was dead.

# 30

## MICHELLE

*12:01 a.m. ET (9:01 p.m. PT)*

*Coltsville, Virginia, NATIC*

Michelle finished up her profile on Reeva Powell. She was about to submit it to the communal databank when she saw that one of the senior researchers had already posted his own workup on Powell, and it was better than Michelle's. He'd scooped up everything Michelle had, and more.

"Great job, Okolo," she whispered to herself.

She gave up on thinking she could contribute to solving the mystery of the hijacking, but she couldn't give up on the kids, on wanting them to be okay, on getting to know them a little bit more.

She had tabs open for each of them. She clicked to Jay Rhee's. His mom had a few friends on Facebook, all from her church group.

She'd posted a picture of a card he'd written her last Mother's Day. He'd written, *Mom, I know you're right (as usual), that going to Hartwell next year will give me a great education in more ways than one. I don't know if I'll fit in there, being the token scholarship kid in the middle of all those rich kids, and I don't know if I even want to be rich myself, but I do know that I want to set things up so that I can take care of you the way you took care of me.*

Tim Cuddy was the most unknowable of the Hartwell crew, or at least the most contradictory. His social media pages were obnoxious—he'd posted a picture of a two-hundred-million-dollar yacht with the text, *This is the one I want, but only if it comes with a private helicopter.*

But there was another side to him—maybe.

Michelle did a search for mentions of him on Facebook. She clicked to the page of the football team's equipment manager, Frazier Smits, a self-proclaimed geek. Frazier suited up for every game as a backup kicker, third-string, but no way was he ever getting onto the field at his size. He couldn't have been more than five feet tall. He'd posted a story a while back about Tim Cuddy:

*Frazier Smits*

*November 11*

*Last night was our last game of the season, and for me, being a senior, it was my last game period. With two seconds left in the fourth quarter, we were up by five touchdowns and soon maybe six. We had the ball at Holy Trinity's nine-yard line. Coach called a timeout and asked Trinity's coach if I could take a shot at a field goal.*

*I was kind of blown away by that, and then I was really blown away when Trinity's coach said he thought that was a nice idea. Everybody agreed there would be no contact on this play, because no way I'd survive even a mediocre tackle, right?*

*Well, one of Trinity's linebackers didn't get the memo.*

*I got off my kick, and even from a few yards away, it barely cleared the crossbar. Still, everybody cheered—everybody except Trinity's outside linebacker, the one who'd been getting outdone all game long. He was a step from drilling me when Timbo leaned into the dude's path. He literally just threw himself in front of me—check out the video below and you'll see that Timbo got knocked unconscious, lights out, full-on concussion. The doc told me when I went to visit Timbo in the hospital after, to yell at him a little for doing that. "You could've been killed," I told him.*

*And here's what Timbo Cuddy said to me: "Smitty, bud, better me than you."*

Michelle's eyes burned. She made a point of trying to end her screen time at midnight, her usual bedtime. She checked the Big Board clock: 12:07 a.m. ET, 9:07 p.m. PT.

# 31

## TIM
### 9:07 p.m. PT
*In the B550*

The nozzle end of the oxygen tank, where the tube hooked into it, was sticking into Tony's skull.

The dude had been so sure of himself just the minute—the *second*—before, and then *bam*, lights out.

Would it be that way for Tim too? Like, one second he'd be here, totally plugged into life, and then blackout? Because it was definite now: They were going to die. He looked at the camera over the cockpit door.

Why wasn't the plane falling out of the sky? Sofia had to know that Tony was dead. Did they have a pact? If one dies, the other keeps going with the plan?

Jay was standing next to Tim, staring at Tony's corpse.

"I believe you now," Tim said. "That you were recruited for pitching. That was some throw."

"We're lucky the tank didn't explode," Brandon said. "If the nozzle had cracked off it, the sudden release of all that pressure would have turned that tank into a missile. It would have been like a bomb going off."

"It's empty," Jay said. "I checked first."

"Jay?" Emily said. "Thank you."

"For what? I just killed somebody."

Tim recognized the look on Jay's face, the same total bewilderment Tim felt the time he'd nearly killed that kid out near the forty-yard line. And Reeva . . .

He couldn't even think about Reeva.

Yes, the look on Jay's face said he was having a hard time coming to grips with the fact that he would never be able to undo the damage he'd caused, the death.

"Jay," Tim said, "I'm sorry."

"For what? You didn't do anything."

He was right. Tim hadn't done anything, and he should have.

He should have tried to get the gun from Tony, but he was afraid.

Why was he still so afraid even now, when they were going to die? He'd had a chance to do the right thing, to die trying, and he'd missed it. Now he was going to die a coward.

"Jay, you had to," Em said.

"It was either him or us," Brandon said, "and we didn't create this situation. I don't think we need to vote this time. We're storming the cockpit. Agreed?"

Even Tim found himself nodding yes. At this point, with Tony dead, what were the chances Sofia would try to finish this thing herself? All that stuff Tony said about the autopilot and the landing on the lake—it had to be a lie. Tony was not to be believed. And what were the chances Sofia wasn't as demented as Tony? Even if she got on the PA and told them they just needed to wait it out, who could believe her? Tim was on board with the others now, 100 percent: This was a suicide mission.

Brandon handed the gun to Emily. She was the best shot of all of them. Her father used to take her hunting. Tim had wanted to come along, but her dad thought *Timbo* was too much of a dumb jock, the kind who'd shoot off his own foot, he'd told Emily.

Em aimed the gun at the keyhole of the cockpit door.

Tim fully expected he was going to be hit with fire extinguisher foam that would torch his face, but he'd still keep going. That cockpit door was going to open one way or another. If Sofia didn't open it, Tim Cuddy would.

Em pulled the trigger. The gun and lock exploded simultaneously.

Tim shoved the others aside. He cranked back the hydraulic lever and pushed through the door.

Both pilot seats were empty.

# 32

## MICHELLE
### 12:10 a.m. ET (9:10 p.m. PT)
*Coltsville, Virginia, NATIC*

Michelle and everybody else in the Big Board room stared at the video the F-22 had just relayed to NATIC. The pilot hadn't been able to see into the cockpit with the lights turned off in there, but he got a solid visual on the passenger cabin. Four of the Hartwell kids looked out the windows, a gun held to Emily Alarcón's head.

Ever the paragon of cool, General Landry let out a long, low whistle when it became clear that the gunman was pilot Tony Blake.

Unaccounted for were Cassie Ando (or at least her body was unaccounted for), the bodyguard Reeva Powell, and the copilot Sofia Palma, presumably in the cockpit.

So now they knew who the bad guy was, or at least who one of them was, but they had no idea what he wanted. That was the critical piece of information, and everybody on the research team was digging wildly for it. One of the techs had commandeered Michelle's desktop to get it running deep database searches on suspected terrorist activity in the California-Mexico border area, where the plane seemed to be headed.

Michelle decided that at this point the most helpful thing she could do was stay out of the way. It was very clear that the senior researchers had this one covered.

Still, she couldn't help but wonder, why?

Why was Blake doing this?

The person who answered that question had a good shot at staying a step ahead of Blake and maybe saving Reeva Powell and the Hartwell friends. The four of them were close to Michelle in age and, now that she'd gotten to know them a little bit online, close to her in another way too: They all had Michelle Okolo–type dreams— big dreams for a bright future, or maybe even a world the slightest bit better than this one.

Edged out of her cubicle, Michelle took her laptop to the coffee area and checked Tony Blake's Facebook page. She had to be missing something. Blake didn't have a lot on his page to sift through. Not a lot of friends, not a lot of posts.

General Landry ordered the F-22s to drop back, but they maintained missile lock on the runaway plane. The B550 was still over the Pacific. It had drifted a hundred and twenty miles off the coast now, but if it made a hard turn and seemed to be heading for a skyscraper or a hospital or even a small town—basically anyplace other than a remote runway or a desert or, in the Barracuda 550's case, a large body of water—then the general had to be ready to shoot it down at a moment's notice.

Michelle clicked to what the FBI had just updated to Tony Blake's file.

Age: fifty-one.

Family history: divorced twice, no kids, briefly was seeing someone he met on Match.com a couple of years ago. That relationship couldn't have been too serious, because when Michelle ran a search on the girlfriend's daughter, she found that while the kid was very active on social media, not once did she mention Blake. Like Sofia Palma, Blake had no parents or siblings. Sofia and Tony were loners, for sure, but Blake was giving off a different kind of loner vibe. Palma had seemed to turn the tragedy of her parents' murder into motivation to succeed in life, maybe to honor them by becoming a successful pilot—or a martyr terrorist. Either way, her profile hinted at a quiet but intense energy, a singleness of purpose, the need to be alone to focus on her mission. Sofia had passion. Michelle wasn't getting that from Tony Blake. His profile, or lack of one, at least in terms of details about things like personal interests or activities outside work, suggested he was a loner because he had given up on people, on life. No family, no love interest, no friends . . . What kept him going? What was he living for, or whom?

Michelle didn't have any great ideas about how to fix this one—not that anyone was asking. Maybe that was a good thing. She most definitely did not want to be put in a position where she could repeat her Kappock, Texas, disaster, except for real this time, and in front of General Landry.

Yeah, best to leave this one to the A-Team.

Michelle looked at the Big Board. The plane was bearing southeast. The engineers anticipated that if it kept up its current trajectory, it would be flying inland somewhere just north of Los Angeles, into Los Padres National Forest.

# 33

## EMILY
### 9:14 p.m. PT
*In the B550*

They found Sofia on the cockpit floor, on her back and very dead. She looked like she'd been that way for a while. The blood had pooled in her hands, deep purple. Her head was at a strange angle, like she was looking over her shoulder too far, too hard, the way you can't do in life unless somebody snaps your neck.

Emily had been thinking all these bad things about her too. It hadn't once crossed her mind that the poor woman could have been innocent, as much a victim as Cassie or Reeva or, at this point, Emily. She tried to close Sofia's eyes, but they wouldn't stay shut. "Tony picked her for her size," Emily said. "He must have been planning this for a long time. He researched the pilots at the staffing agency, and then he asked for Sofia specifically. She was tiny. He knew she would be easy to overpower when the time came."

Brandon nodded, but he didn't say anything. Like Emily, he seemed to be having a hard time taking his eyes off the corpse—the fourth. Half the people who'd gotten on the plane were dead. But Sofia's death was hitting Emily the hardest, even more than Cassie's for now. "The poor girl was just trying to get by," she said. *Trying to make a living in a field dominated by men,* she thought. Or at least Emily had never seen a pilot who wasn't a dude. *She probably figured this was her big break, getting to copilot a private jet.*

"Nobody's been flying the plane for a while now," Jay said, "so I guess that means it's programmed to fly a certain course."

"It can fly itself with autopilot—I'll buy that," Brandon said. "But do we believe Tony that this thing can land itself on a lake?"

"It says it can on the Barracuda website," Jay said.

"With people in it?" Brandon said. "I'd feel better if we at least had an idea whether or not the autopilot plans to take us to Pyramid Lake."

Emily studied the plane's control panel, the tens if not hundreds of switches and buttons, the multiple screens and gauges.

They looked for a manual, but of course there was none.

They had no way to contact air traffic control either. Every time Emily clicked the radio microphone, a message came onscreen:

INVALID ACTION.

ACCESS DENIED.

The air force must've been having the same problem, because no audio was coming into the cockpit.

Tony had thought of everything, it seemed. He'd even come up with a plan to stop the Hartwell kids from taking control of the plane in case he couldn't prevent them from getting into the cockpit.

Tim tried to get control of the plane in his own way, by yanking as hard as he could on the steering column, but it wouldn't budge.

"Don't break it, Tim," Emily said.

Tim kept trying anyway.

"Tim, if you do manage to get control of it, who flies it?" Brandon said.

Tim stopped yanking on the steering mechanism.

The flight control screen blinked every two seconds to remind everyone that the plane was on AUTOPILOT—AUTOPILOT— AUTOPILOT. They were flying blind.

Emily's mind was beginning to play tricks on her: She thought she heard a buzz, the kind a phone on mute makes to indicate an incoming text. She checked her phone, but no, no text, no bars, no ability to call out for help. It had to be coming from the control panel, but the noise seemed to be coming from behind her.

There it was again—*buzz*, seemingly louder now with everyone despairing and silent.

Brandon, Jay, Tim checked their phones.

Nothing, no cell service, no Wi-Fi, no texts.

*Buzz.*

Emily followed the noise into the passenger cabin and traced it to Reeva's body.

*Buzz*, louder now.

Emily patted down Reeva's pockets, then the empty gun holster. There was a hidden pocket, and inside was a second phone, Reeva's backup, just as Granny Smith green as the first one Tony had destroyed, and just as jacked-up with a direct satellite link.

Emily read the text stream. "They're not telling us to stand by anymore. They want to know our status."

"Em?" Brandon said.

"Stop crying, right?"

"Cry all you want, but I think you might want to text them back."

# 34

## MICHELLE
### *12:30 a.m. ET (9:30 p.m. PT)*
*Coltsville, Virginia, NATIC*

Reeva Powell had been unresponsive to NATIC's texts for a while when the text came in from Emily Alarcón. Everybody in the Big Board room cheered. Emily's words appeared on the movie theater–size screen in real time.

```
THIS IS EMILY.
REEVA IS DEAD.
```

Nobody seemed surprised by that news, but Michelle heard sighs. Those ended when the next news came in:

TONY IS DEAD.

TONY KILLED SOFIA.

THERE'S NO ONE TO FLY THE PLANE.

THE PLANE IS ON AUTOPILOT.

WE CAN'T DISENGAGE.

HELP.

"Okay, plug in the engineers and let's get these kids home safe," General Landry said.

While Major Serrano's comm team got the story, text by text, line by line, of exactly what had happened up there in the B550, the engineers were texting back to the plane with code to hack the autopilot. If they could override it and reestablish the plane's onboard communication link, they could program the plane to land anywhere they wanted, like at a regional airport where clearing the air traffic would be much easier.

"Estimated time needed for recovery of the plane's flight control system?" Major Serrano called out.

"Ninety minutes to two hours?" the head engineer said.

"Statement or question?" the major said.

The NATIC flight trajectory specialists ran those numbers and figured out that the takeover of the plane's flight controls would happen between ten and forty minutes *after* the plane was due to land on Pyramid Lake, if it was in fact going to land there.

The negotiators and SWAT team were being deployed to the lake in case Tony Blake was telling the truth. Nobody knew what the chances of that were, just like nobody knew Blake. He kept his mind offline.

But everybody kept a little treasure somewhere. Memories of better times, like the thank-you letter your dad wrote you after you knit him the saddest-looking wool tie for Father's Day, the letter that said the proudest accomplishment of his life was that he and your mom had raised a kind person, and who could wish for a more spectacular daughter? Michelle stashed that one in her keepsake box, once home to the pair of Nike trainers Dad got her for her twelfth birthday so they could run together. He died before she could break them in.

Where did Tony Blake hide his Nike box, the one with the memories he couldn't bear to lose?

The FBI was in his apartment in New York right now, running scans on his laptop. More than his computer, they wanted to hack his phone. That, of course, was up in the plane, and it was locked with Blake's passcode. The NATIC techs were trying to help the Hartwell crew crack the code, but so far no luck.

Major Serrano came into the coffee area to refill her cup. Behind her, General Landry stood and stretched and called out to her assistant, "The jets are in position?"

"Yes, ma'am."

"Good."

Michelle turned to the major and whispered, "She's shooting it down?"

"If that plane deviates from the course Blake laid out, she has to," the major said.

So far the plane was following the flight path that Tony Blake had described to Michelle's Hartwell crew. Okay, so maybe they weren't her crew, but she knew enough about them at this point that if they didn't make it, she would feel she'd lost some friends. She really hoped they cracked that phone. She was less interested in Blake's communications than she was in getting a peek at his photos.

She checked the time clock. The plane was supposed to land at Pyramid Lake around 10:40 p.m. PT, an hour from now.

Why of all places would you land a plane on a lake? If you were looking for a desolate place, there were plenty of rarely used landing strips in the desert. What was it about the water that had drawn Tony Blake to it?

# 35

## EMILY
### 9:40 p.m. PT
*In the B550*

The four of them were crammed into the cockpit. The boys were under the dashboard with their phone lights, pulling out fuses and switchboxes and who knew what else. Emily read out the directions from the engineers on the ground. NATIC had opened up a line of communication for Reeva's phone through another, more powerful satellite, and now Emily was able to send very low-res pictures of the control panel screens to the engineers.

Seeing the flight control panel being dismantled, wires everywhere, was unsettling, but Emily didn't have time to freak out. She had a second text stream going with a whole other group of NATIC engineers. They wanted her to get into Tony's phone, and they were feeding her long strings of numbers they hoped would bypass Tony's password. Now they were sending a text that they needed her to get Tony's credit cards, his IDs, any receipts he might have on him.

"Uh, guys? They want me to search Tony's pants. I can't do it alone."

"Why do they want you to dig into his *pants*?" Tim said.

"For his *wallet*. I binge-watched every *Walking Dead* episode this summer. I've seen what happens when you start rummaging through the pockets of dead people."

"Em, suck it up," Tim said, wedged into a slot beneath the control panel. "Just go get it. He's not going to fight you, I promise."

"Jay, please?" she said.

"Let's bring the gun, just in case," Jay said.

They went to where they had laid out the four bodies. They had dropped a towel over the top half of Tony's body to hide his face. His hands stuck out from underneath the towel.

His hands.

Emily gave herself a second to shudder before she forced herself to grab Tony's right index finger and press it onto his phone's home button.

The phone opened.

"Wow, you're awesome," Jay said. "I thought you needed to be alive to open a phone with your fingerprint—like have electricity in you."

"Apparently not. NATIC wants to look at his photos, but how do we send them when his phone is just a regular old Droid, no cell signal or anything? I mean, it's definitely not military grade, like Reeva's, with the satellite thing."

"Exactly," Jay said. He opened the photo album on Tony's phone and took a picture of the screen with Reeva's phone. Now that the engineers had opened up a new satellite link with a wider data pipeline, they could text the pictures, one by one, to NATIC.

"Wow, *you're* awesome," Emily said. She looked back toward the cockpit. All she could see of Tim was his leg, sticking out from under the control panel.

He called out, "Em, I got that DC 4A wire free from the whatever the heck you call it! We're getting there. We're gonna have this plane under our thumb soon. What's next?"

# 36

## MICHELLE
### 12:56 a.m. ET (9:56 p.m. PT)
*Coltsville, Virginia, NATIC*

Michelle snatched the pictures from the server one by one as Emily texted them down from the plane. She lined them up on her screen against Tony Blake's Facebook feed.

Nobody looked familiar. Most of the pictures on Blake's phone were group shots from aviation conferences, or scenery from the cockpit window, clouds that looked like mountains, mountains that looked like ocean waves.

One picture from Blake's phone kept pulling at her, the first one the Hartwell crew beamed down and the last picture Blake's phone had taken. Blake was in the cockpit with a stuffed animal in his lap, a very pretty horse. Blake's face in the picture was strange.

He was grinning, but his eyes were filled with . . .

With what?

It went beyond sadness. It was the same thing Michelle saw in Cassie's eyes and in her own eyes now, in the reflection of the mini-refrigerator glass directly across from her, on the other side of the coffee area table. The kind of loss that never goes away.

Michelle was pretty sure all the other researchers—the *real* ones—were investigating this picture too, so there was no need to flag it for Major Serrano, probably.

Still, though.

Still.

Michelle went to Major Serrano's desk. The boss was swamped, reading two iPads at once with her adjutant waiting for direction. "What's up, Michelle?" the major said without looking up from her reports.

Michelle showed her the picture of Blake and the stuffed horse. Cassie Ando huddled with Blake. She was giving the peace sign and the wink of course, and sticking her tongue out the side of her mouth. "Major, is there any way you can ask our communications point person to text Emily about this stuffed horse?"

The major looked at the picture. "Where you going with this one, Okolo?"

"I really don't know. I just have this gut feeling it's a clue of some kind."

The major frowned. "We want to keep that comm line clear of all but absolutely necessary transmission." She glanced up and did a double-take on Michelle. "How strong a gut feeling?"

"Like I might throw up."

Major Serrano nodded to her adjutant. "Get me everything you can about the pony."

# 37

# BRANDON

*10:02 p.m. PT*

*In the B550*

"Next?" Brandon said. He was on his back, under the dashboard. He was holding the G-144 wire, or maybe it was the G-145, and now he was waiting for direction from NATIC.

Emily checked the text stream. "They want to know about the horse. The picture where Cass and Tony are with the stuffed animal Cass gave him. All I know is, he said he was giving it to his goddaughter."

"Then text them that," Brandon said. He checked his watch. They had forty minutes, supposedly, before the plane hit the lake. *Less* than forty minutes.

To hack into a super-sophisticated aeronautical operating system.

And the stuffed animal thing—asking about a stuffed horse seemed way off the mark at this point.

Was NATIC giving up on the idea that they would be able to take over the plane's flight controls?

Were they trying to get whatever information they could about Tony and his crime before the plane went down and all the evidence turned to fire and ash?

Brandon hauled himself out from under the dashboard, never mind the rewiring NATIC wanted him to do. He sat back in the pilot's seat.

"You're giving up?" Tim said.

"Brand?" Em said.

"We have to get off this plane," he said.

Tim laughed.

"I'm serious," Brandon said. "It's not going to land at Pyramid Lake, much less on it."

Jay pointed to the flight path screen NATIC had gotten online for them. "The autopilot's following the exact flight path Tony told us about."

"For now," Brandon said.

"Dude, the ETA clock says we'll be there in thirty-seven minutes."

"That's still plenty of time to change course. Look, why would Tony have given us that information? He was covering his bases. If somehow we were able to incapacitate him and hack the communications system and make contact with NATIC, we'd tell them what he told us, that he programmed the plane to land at Pyramid Lake. This was Tony's insurance policy. If he wasn't around to control the flow of information, he would leave us with bad information to relay to NATIC, a decoy to take the focus off his intended target."

"So then what's the real target?" Tim said.

"I don't know, a condo tower, a retirement community. Does it matter? Do you want to stick around to find out?"

"Bro, what choice do we have?"

"Brand, just hear me out here for a second," Em said. "I've been going back and forth about whether or not Tony was telling the truth, but now NATIC is backing him up, right? They told us the plane is best in its class for emergency water landings."

"They got that off the same website Jay did—the manufacturer's website. And anyway, what does that mean, 'best in class'? If the average plane has a terrible chance of making a water landing and this one's chances are better than terrible, what good does that do us? We're cruising at more than five hundred miles an hour. Even if it slows down to a hundred and fifty by the time we land, the friction of the water is going to tear open the bottom of the plane, and once that happens, the plane stops short. I don't care how strong those seat belts are, our bodies are not going from a hundred and fifty miles an hour to zero and staying in one piece. So, unless we can get manual control of the plane and get some serious coaching from NATIC on how to land it, as in on *land*, then we have to get off the plane."

"And you don't think we'll get manual control of the plane?" Emily said.

"Not in thirty-four minutes." Brandon nodded to the ETA clock. "Thirty-*three* minutes to Pyramid Lake now, if it is actually landing there."

"Okay, Brand, so, what—after all this we're just gonna do a suicide jump?" Tim said.

"Brandon's right," Emily said. "We're jumping. Guys, hello, Cassie's parachute, the one that saved her when she fell off the slackline? There was that backup too, tucked away in the gear pile, in case any of us decided to go Casserole-crazy and go out on the line with her."

"You mean the parachutes stowed away in the *cargo* compartment in the *bottom* of the plane?" Tim said. "The one we can't get to without climbing *outside* to the cargo hold door, which is screwed shut, by the way, all at five hundred and whatever miles an hour?"

"Even if we could get to them, what good are two chutes?" Jay said.

"Two people for each chute," Brandon said. "I helped Cassie repack that chute. We needed four hands to roll it tight enough to get it into the backpack. Those chutes are military. They're rated to accommodate the weight of a paratrooper with full gear, and the gear could be up to a hundred fifty pounds. I was with Cass when she was shopping for them last spring. Figure each chute can carry four hundred pounds, give or take."

"Let it be give," Emily said. She pulled out her phone calculator. "Let's go, fess up your poundage, men. Brand?"

"One sixty-five."

"One seventy, one seventy-five," Jay said.

"I'm one forty-five," Emily said. "Tim?"

He hesitated, staring at Em.

"What's up?" Em said.

"It's just . . . I don't know, it's embarrassing." Tim looked wounded.

"Timmy seriously, what's wrong?"

"I was two forty last time I weighed myself, but I'm pretty sure I lost like at least five pounds since then."

"Okay, so it's me and Jay on one chute, and Tim and Em on the other, with pounds to spare," Brandon said. He hoped he was remembering right about those parachute ratings.

"Now all we have to do is get into the cargo hold," Em said.

"Not a problem," Jay said. He held up the full oxygen tank.

Brandon smiled, but not for long. He checked his wristwatch. "We have nineteen minutes to get off this plane."

"The ETA clock says we have thirty-one before we hit Pyramid Lake," Tim said.

Brandon pointed to the flight path screen. "We have to jump while we're over the water. Once the plane's over land, NATIC can't shoot it down without killing people on the ground."

"Jay, how are you going to use an oxygen tank to make a hole in a metal floor?" Em said.

"The hole's already there," Jay said. "We just have to make it bigger."

# 38

## JAY
### 10:11 p.m. PT
*In the B550*

They crowded into the kitchen area and stood over the hole where the sink drain had been before they tore out the pipes to get at the refrigerator.

The hole was about six inches in diameter. Jay slipped the oxygen tank halfway into the hole. The tank didn't fit in there tightly enough. Without any kind of support it would fall through the hole, into the belly of the plane. It needed to stay at the level of the floor. Jay wrapped a towel around the tank to create a snug fit, and this time it stuck just right in the hole, about half of it above the level of the floor, half of it below. The tank was full of $O_2$ at two thousand pounds of pressure per square inch, the gauge said.

"You're gonna hammer the neck off?" Tim said.

"We can't be near that thing when it blows," Brandon said. "It'll be a fire bomb."

"Exactly," Emily said. "We just need to get the oxygen in the tank hot enough to expand, and the tank will blow on its own." She held up Reeva's gun. "One hot bullet sinking through the aluminum in that tank wall is all the heat and spark we'll need. Take cover, boys," Em said.

They lined up behind Em near the front of the plane, as far away from the tank as they could be, hiding behind a barricade they made of the torn-up kitchen counter.

Em lined up her shot. Jay winced even before she pulled the trigger.

*Bang—*

*Ping—*

*Crack—*

*Whoosh—*

The sounds seemed to come all at once.

Em was dead-on with her aim, but the bullet ricocheted off the tank and into a double-paned Plexiglas window. The inside window completely blew out, but the outside Plexiglas held, except for a spiderweb crack. For a little hole it sure made a lot of noise. The air pressure differential was crazy, and the higher-pressure air in the plane was squeezing out of that tiny hole in the glass fast. Jay's ears ached.

Em lined up again.

*Bang—*

Nothing else this time, no *ping, crack, whoosh.* The bullet was stuck in the side of the aluminum tank.

"We have three bullets left," Em said.

Jay looked out the window. The lights of the coast seemed to be getting brighter, closer, a definite sprawl of gold that had to be Los Angeles.

"We have fifteen minutes to make this happen and get out of the plane," Brandon said.

The next bullet was a miss, and then the second-to-last bullet—

*BANG.*

# 39

# MICHELLE
## 1:13 a.m. ET (10:13 p.m. PT)
### Coltsville, Virginia, NATIC

There was silence in the Big Board room as everyone watched the video replay on the screen. The F-22 tailing the rogue B550 had been live streaming from its vantage point a few hundred yards away from the plane.

The B550 had been proceeding smoothly on course for its supposed landing on Pyramid Lake. The plane was a dark silhouette in the moonlit sky, until there was a blinding orange-white flash in the middle of the plane, and the passenger cabin lights went out.

The same NATIC folks who'd groaned the first time they saw the video groaned even louder now.

"Not good," somebody said.

Uh, *no*. Still, whatever had happened in the passenger cabin seemed to have had no effect on the plane's flight controls. The B550 continued to hold true to its trajectory toward Los Padres National Forest.

"They'll be over land in about fourteen minutes, General," Landry's assistant said.

The general nodded. "If they're still alive. See if the F-22 can get a closer look at what's going on in there. If those kids are confirmed dead, I want that plane taken down now. Otherwise, how are we looking for a landing on Pyramid Lake?"

The captain who led the team that projected trajectories said, "All signs are the plane is right on the money for the lake, General."

Then the Big Board lit up with a text from the plane:

```
WE'RE ALL FINE. WE'RE GOING TO JUMP. WE
HAVE PARACHUTES.
OR WE WILL IN A FEW MINUTES.
```

"Somebody read that out loud to me," the general said.

Somebody did.

"Tell them their chances are better if they stay in the plane," the general said. She called out to her statistician, "Michael, just for kicks, can you give me a feasibility workup on their chances of surviving a parachute jump from where they are? Let's figure out how hard it'll be to clear the intake of the jet's engines, where they might land, if they'll land alive, and if they do, whether we'll get to them in time before they freeze, drown, or become shark bait."

"You got it, ma'am."

Michelle tracked the red and blue dots on the Big Board. The F-22s were right on the B550's tail, ready to shoot it down.

General Landry called to Major Serrano, "Let's tell those 22s to spread out a little bit. I don't want any accidents up there. We're still looking good for Pyramid Lake. If that bird holds true to her trajectory, she'll come in overland at Lompoc, then it's all national forest to the lake. Almost zero population density the whole way. Even if the plane crashes or we shoot it down, we'd have a better chance of electing rational people to Congress than we would killing anybody on the ground. But if that plane starts to drift toward the city, I want the Raptors to take it out before it breaches Greater Los Angeles airspace."

"Gotcha, General," Major Serrano said.

The major was relaying the general's orders to the F-22 pilots when the big screen lit up with another text from the plane.

IS IT TRUE THAT IF IT LOOKS LIKE WE'RE NOT GOING TO LAND ON THE LAKE AFTER ALL, THAT YOU HAVE TO SHOOT US DOWN?

That stopped the room cold. Michelle noticed the general was looking at her, maybe because Michelle was pretty much the same age as the kids up in that plane.

*Please don't lie to them,* Michelle thought. *Please, give them the information they need to decide for themselves whether or not they should jump or stay.*

"General?" Major Serrano said. "What do you want to tell them?"

"The truth. They have a right to know." General Landry frowned. "Keep it short. Answer yes. Ask them to stay on the plane. At this point, all signs are that they're going to land on the lake." She seemed to sink back in her chair a little when the next text came in.

PLEASE TELL OUR FAMILIES WE LOVE THEM.

And then another one:

THIS IS FOR MRS. RHEE. JAY SAYS: THANK YOU
FOR WORKING SO HARD TO GIVE ME OPPORTUNITIES
TO LIVE AN AMAZING LIFE. THE BEST PART OF
THE WHOLE THING WAS, I GOT TO BE YOUR SON.

"I'd like to meet that young man someday," the general said. "Let's do every last thing we can to make that happen, if not for me, then Mrs. Rhee."

Michelle kept going back to that picture of Tony Blake with the stuffed horse. She checked his Facebook for any signs of his goddaughter, but so far there was nothing.

# 40

## EMILY
*10:16 p.m. PT*
*In the B550*

Emily's eardrums were still ringing. When the oxygen tank exploded, the blast cracked two windows. The air whistled in, or maybe it was whistling out, in one long shriek.

The fire flash burned the ceiling over where the tank blew up. Pieces of the tank had blown everywhere. The shrapnel was stuck in the seats and walls, the countertop the kids used as a shield. The air inside the cabin had gotten very hot for a few seconds, and then it became a lot colder. The four of them were red and sweaty and shivering. The tank had blown the hole in the floor open a little wider, but not wide enough for a body to get through. Not yet anyway.

Tim attacked one of the metal beams sticking up from the hole in the floor. As the boys helped him bend it back to widen the hole, Emily tried to gather her thoughts for the next text down to NATIC. The explosion had been so loud, and now her ears were more than ringing, burning down deep into her throat, where a lump was forming.

*Do. Not. Cry*, she told herself. *Not yet.*

She had to get them out, the last words she might ever get to say to her parents.

FOR MR. AND MRS. ALARCÓN: I WANT YOU TO KNOW THAT RIGHT NOW, IN THIS CRAZY MOMENT, I'M SO GRATEFUL, MOM AND DAD. I'M WITH MY FRIENDS, AND YOU GUYS ARE WITH ME IN MY HEART. I LOVE YOU ALWAYS.

"Go, go, go, go, go!" Tim said.

They had widened the hole in the floor just enough so Jay could drop into the belly of the plane with his phone light. A minute later he was passing the two parachute packs up through the hole to Tim.

The plane was seven minutes from reaching the coast now, according to the countdown clock Em had programmed into Reeva's phone.

The four friends agreed they would wait for word from the general before they jumped. If the general was sure—or as sure as she could be—that the plane was going to land on the lake, they would wait it out in the plane. The people on the ground had texted some interesting stats a minute ago. The chances of surviving a water landing in a B550 were a little better than 74 percent. The chances of jumping from the plane, avoiding being incinerated by the jet's engines, then surviving a parachute fall at night into the ocean were 48 percent. On the other hand, the general had told them that once the plane was over Los Padres National Forest, if it started to drift toward civilization, the F-22s would shoot it down, and nobody had to tell Emily that the chances of surviving that one were nonexistent.

The general said she would give the kids a ten-second warning before she had the plane shot down. They could stay in the plane, and the explosion would kill them instantly. Or, they could take their chances at a jump while the plane was still over the forest. At that point the plane would be at a much lower altitude. This, along with the fact that the Hartwell crew would be jumping into a forest full of pine trees in the middle of the night, put their chances of survival at less than 5 percent.

Still, a 5 percent chance was infinitely better than 0 percent, which were Emily's odds of surviving a plane crash. She was not going to die on this plane, to have her body burned to goop, unrecognizable as human. Better to die in a fall, out in the open air, under the stars. Emily had to be ready to jump no matter what. The boys were in agreement with her.

She watched as Brandon, Tim, and Jay put on their inflatable life preserver vests. Brandon and Jay tied themselves back to back with seat belt straps. Jay wore the pack on his chest.

"Make sure you're looking toward the sky when you pull the rip cord," Brandon said.

Emily got the picture: If Jay was looking down when he pulled the cord, the parachute, exploding from the pack, would break his neck.

Jay and Brand were ready to go and waited by the passenger cabin door. All they had to do was pull that lever. The door would blow open, and they would be sucked out of the plane.

Tim was oddly quiet as he strapped Emily into an inflatable life preserver vest, and then, on top of that, the parachute pack. He was soaked with sweat, even though it was cold in the plane with the air screaming in through the cracks in the windows. He'd given it his all, tearing up the floor. He'd given his all before that too, when he charged the cockpit door.

"Tim?" Emily said. "I'm sorry."

"For what?"

"Just, thank you. You're awesome. You *are*."

"This is all gonna be over really soon, Em. It's going to work out okay." He kissed her, and it felt the way it had when they started hanging out the year before—a rushing thrill that radiated from her heart, spreading everywhere. It felt right, like the time he opened up and told her that his biggest fear was he wouldn't figure it out in time—figure out how to go from being a confused, frightened kid to a good man, somebody who actually had something to give to the world. Well, that was actually his second-biggest fear, he'd said. The first was that he'd lose her friendship.

She hugged him, and he pulled a seat belt strap around them to bind them together.

# 41

## MICHELLE
### 1:22 a.m. ET (10:22 p.m. PT)
*Coltsville, Virginia, NATIC*

The picture on Michelle's laptop screen was of a little girl, maybe five or six. She was waving into the camera, smiling. She had long brown hair and big brown eyes. This was Tony's goddaughter, Patrice Mixtos.

Michelle had run a search of Blake's Facebook with the word *goddaughter* without success, but when she typed *godfather*, the page jumped down to a post from five years ago.

One of Blake's few Facebook friends, Carrie Mixtos, had written, *Love to the greatest godfather on the occasion of Patrice's tenth birthday!* And Tony had replied, *Love back.*

Then Michelle had clicked to Carrie Mixtos's page and to the date she had posted to Tony's page and found that picture of Patrice.

Why on Patrice's tenth birthday would Carrie post a picture of Patrice when she was five?

Michelle looked at the countdown clock to when the plane would be approaching the coast and the general would have to make the call on whether or not to tell the Hartwell kids to jump and then ten seconds after that, maybe give the order to shoot down the plane. The clock read, 4:31, 4:30, 4:29 . . .

Google search: *Patrice Mixtos.*

Wait, Patrice was dead? Her obituary in a local Kansas newspaper said she'd died when she was five. Leukemia, likely brought on by a chemical spill that had seeped into the groundwater by her house. Other kids in the area had gotten sick too.

Patrice would have been fifteen now, Cassie's age.

According to Emily Alarcón, Tony Blake said he was going to give that stuffed horse to Patrice. But she'd died ten years earlier.

3:53, 3:52 . . .

Michelle googled: *Patrice Mixtos Ando.*

That was it. The phosphorous plant leak that killed Patrice was owned by Merit Industries, which was owned by Ando Chemical. Merit was located in Urmansville, Kansas, a rural community in the southwest part of the state. Urmansville rang a bell from the FBI file on Blake. That was Tony's hometown.

Michelle scanned the court case settlement, which was public information. Ando Chemical admitted no wrongdoing but paid ten million dollars to Patrice's mom to settle the suit.

2:59, 2:58 . . .

Michelle found a follow-up article dated four years ago that said Carrie Mixtos had committed suicide, leaving what was left of the money she'd won in the court case settlement to cancer research.

Blake was more than angry. He was delusional. The kind of delusional where he was willing to spend years quietly plotting revenge against the people responsible for that chemical spill.

2:00. The board flashed and an alarm chirped. Michelle looked around the room. People were running, yelling, but she couldn't hear them. The alarm sound faded too as Michelle concentrated on her laptop screen. All she could hear was the sound of her fingers tapping the laptop keys.

She googled: *Ando Los Angeles.*

About 16,000 results (0.14 seconds).

1:51 . . .

Next she tried: *Ando Los Angeles plant factory warehouse refinery manufacturer.*

The top hit: Lackland Industrial, largest manufacturer of chlorine gas in the continental US, a subsidiary of Ando Chemical Inc.

On Google Maps the Lackland chlorine plant was located at the northern edge of Los Angeles County, in Los Trujillos, just inland from the coast and less than half a mile from the western edge of Los Padres National Forest. At the coastline, with a sharp turn off course, the hijacked plane could fly right into that refinery in less than a minute.

She googled: *weather Los Angeles*.

With the northwest winds, the cloud of chlorine gas would be all across Los Angeles within minutes. Millions could die. Millions of kids Patrice's age. There was no settling *that* court case. That one would put Ando Chemical and a lot of other chemical companies out of business, and maybe even get the government to enforce a whole bunch of laws that would ensure this kind of thing would never happen again—kids getting poisoned, especially poor kids who lived near industrial plants.

0:02, 0:01, 0:00.

"General, it's time to make the call," Major Serrano said. "Do the kids jump or sit tight?"

"The plane's still on course for Pyramid Lake?"

"Affirmative."

"Good," the general said. "All right, then, let's get word to our young friends up there that we advise they stay put, and be sure to buckle up for that landing on the water. Tell them we'll have rescue boats on the lake, waiting for them, and we're hoping that they—"

"No, ma'am, they have to jump," Michelle said, realizing too late that she had just cut off a United States Air Force general.

"Excuse me?"

"Michelle!" Major Serrano said.

"The plane, ma'am," Michelle said. "They have to get out of there. You have to shoot it down now. It's going to crash-land at Los Trujillos, into a chlorine gas plant. It's just inland, just north of LA.

I expect any second now the plane is going to make a sharp turn toward it. With the summer winds—"

"You're sure about this?" the general said. Her face was placid. She could have been asking for another cup of coffee.

"Yes, ma'am. Tony Blake's goddaughter was—"

"We don't have time for explanations," the general said. "I just need to know: Are you sure?"

Michelle was not sure, not at all. She closed her eyes to run the two scenarios through her mind. If the Hartwell crew died in the jump and the plane ended up staying on course for Pyramid Lake, Michelle Okolo would have killed four kids. Then again, if she was right, and the plane suddenly hooked north for the Lackland Plant, it would have to be shot down, and the kids, even if they could get out of the plane with a ten-second warning, would be parachuting at an extremely low altitude. Even if their chutes did open in time, with the onshore wind drift, they would be blown into the city, most likely onto the freeways. No way they'd survive a landing on a busy LA freeway, and they'd kill people on the ground with the traffic accidents they would cause by making the cars and semis swerve.

"Michelle?" Major Serrano said.

Michelle opened her eyes and looked directly into General Landry's. "Yes, ma'am. I'm sure."

The general nodded. "Major Serrano, let's get word to our friends that they need to get out of that plane *now*."

# 42

## TIM
**10:28 p.m. PT**

*In the B550*

"We have to go," Em said after reading NATIC's *jump immediately* text to the others. "*Now.*"

Now?

*I can do this*, Tim thought. *I can. I'm not afraid. Don't think, just do. Better me than you.*

He couldn't stop looking into Emily's eyes. All the times they'd spent together came back at once, flashes of memory, their first kiss after sharing a milkshake, her kissing the strawberry mustache from Tim's lip, so cold and warm at the same time, so sweet.

"Tim, c'mon, let's *go*," she said. "You okay?"

He nodded. Yes, he was okay. He kissed her one last time.

The four of them were in front of the emergency exit, a little ahead of the jet's left side engine. "Remember to drop instead of jump," Brandon said. "If you jump out too far, the engine's intake will suck you into the turbo fan."

"Got it," Tim said. "Sliced Timbo, not what we're looking for." He clapped Brandon's shoulder.

Brand was trembling. "See you in the water, Tim."

"You bet." Tim felt oddly calm as he watched Brandon yank on the emergency exit door's lever.

The door blew off the plane, and Brand and Jay were sucked into the sky. They dropped out of view so fast their screams fell away in less than a second. They'd cleared the engine. Whatever else happened, they were out of the plane.

Now Tim and Em were at the exit. With one hand, Tim held on to the door frame.

"Ready?" Em said.

"I'm ready."

She hugged him, locking her hands behind his neck. He wanted so much to hug her back, with both arms. His left arm was around her waist, but he had to keep holding on to the door frame with his right hand, his stronger hand.

"Tim, let go!" she said.

He did—of her. The wind rushing past the door pulled her out of the plane, but he was still bracing himself in the doorway. Her arms around his neck were their only connection. Her eyes went wide when she realized what he'd done. He'd only pretended to tie himself to her with the seat belt: He'd left the buckle undone.

"Tim, what are you doing? *Please*, come with me!"

"The parachute, Em. I helped Brand and Cassie bag it, and I saw the label. It said, 'Chute will fail over three hundred seventy-five pounds.' Em, I'm two sixty. It won't hold both of us." He pried her hands from his neck.

"No! Tim!" She held on to the door frame. "We stay together!"

"Only in our hearts this time, Em." He forced her hand from the door frame.

She flew downward into the dark and way too fast. She had dropped out of view in less than a second. He searched the sky below, but she was gone. He looked up. The stars were out, and they were so bright up here, above the light pollution of the city.

He found the Appaloosa horse in one of the seats and brought it back to Cassie. He tucked it under her arm, and then he sat next to her and held her hand. It was cold, stiff, dry, but he remembered when he and Cassie were in first grade, when they'd walk home together, and their mothers told them to be sure to hold each other's hands and look out for each other.

He wished he had Reeva's phone, but Emily had taken it with her, wrapped in a candy bag with a Ziploc top to help NATIC track them down when they hit the water. He probably should've sent a message to his parents, to let them know how he felt about them and how he felt about everything. Emily would tell them, though, how he found himself right before he died, found his purpose. He wasn't scared anymore. He felt completely free.

The blast was coming, any second. "We go together, Cass," he said. "We'll go holding hands." But then it hit him hard that Cassie would want him to die flying. He could almost hear her infectious, way-too-loud laugh, which could turn into a giddy howl sometimes, like now. It was almost as if Cassie's spirit was laughing through him, with him.

He ran for the exit, and he kept running, straight out into the sky, reaching for the moon.

# 43

## EMILY
### 10:33 p.m. PT

*Somewhere over the Pacific Ocean, off the coast of Los Angeles*

Em was sure her neck had snapped when the chute opened. The sudden slowdown of her falling made her feel she was flying upward. But no, she was still falling, and fast. Her neck wasn't broken after all, she realized, as she looked left and right, searching the sky for the other parachute. She couldn't find it. She was so alone.

Above her, the doomed plane grew smaller. Then it made a very sudden turn off course, away from Los Padres National Forest. It seemed to be going into a dive toward lights on the coast.

So in the end it was a suicide mission. How had NATIC figured it out, and just in time?

In time for her anyway, and maybe for Brandon and Jay, if their chute had held out. But not for Tim.

"Tim," she whispered. Her tears ran cold and upward from her eyes, she was dropping toward the ocean so quickly. She became aware of a pink glow above her and off to her right—a red glow now and brighter, hot red. She rubbed her eyes to clear her vision.

Two smoky red streaks raced toward the plane, and then it was just a fireball falling into the ocean—except the smoke from the blast grew upward like a gray hand reaching out over the city.

# 44

## MICHELLE
*1:35 a.m. ET*

*Coltsville, Virginia, NATIC*

They had seen it all on the huge screen, the F-22's POV as the plane exploded. Everyone was silent. Michelle wondered if anybody else could hear her heart pounding.

General Landry's assistant was wearing her headset. She nodded to the general. "Plane is confirmed neutralized and falling into the water, General."

General Landry nodded. "Do we have a visual on the parachutes?"

"Yes, ma'am. Confirming the two chutes have cleared the explosion, still in descent toward the water. We have tracer lights on them. Their projected landing is a mile offshore, and . . . wait . . . yes, the bodies are tight in descent, no loose limbs."

The general smiled, and for the first time Michelle saw Landry's teeth. "Which means they're holding tight to each other, probably kicking and screaming bloody blue murder as they fall," the general said. "Yup, they made it."

Now came the cheers, the claps on Michelle's back.

"Woo-hoo, Michelle!"

"Good call, Okolo!"

"Good luck trying to get her to make you a coffee now."

"Can heroes even pour coffee?"

Somebody poured Sprite over her head.

Michelle laughed, but very quickly that turned to crying, and then sobbing. She wasn't sure why. Major Serrano pulled her in close. "You're okay," the major said. "You're just fine."

She felt a hand on her shoulder. "Stop crying," General Landry said. "Shoulders back. Breathe."

"Yes, ma'am." Michelle did as she was told, trying to catch her breath, to slow down her heart. If it kept pumping this fast, she was sure to die or at least pass out, and she wasn't doing either before she got that stupid letter of recommendation.

"You did well."

"Thank you, ma'am."

"You're a senior in high school, starting next week. That right, Okolo?"

"Yes, ma'am."

"What are your hopes in the way of college?"

"My dream is to attend the United States Air Force Academy, ma'am."

"That little old school out there in Colorado Springs? Yes, I believe I have heard of that one. Excellent. In fact, if memory serves, I might happen to know one or two of the folks who run the place, and I can't think of a better spot for a fine young analyst like you." She turned to her assistant. "Put General Rodriguez at the top of my call list for tomorrow."

"Yes, ma'am." The assistant winked at Michelle.

"Major Serrano," the general said, "let's fish our Hartwell Academy friends out of the drink there. Let's get them dry and warm and bring them home."

"You got it, General."

"Unless you need me, I'll be heading home myself, then," the general said. "The poor dog will be cross-legged by now, holding it in the whole night."

"My apologies to Ike, ma'am," the major said.

"Indeed." The general was at the door when she seemed to remember something. "Okolo, it occurs to me just now, I do have one very big concern about you."

Michelle lifted her head high to mask the sinking feeling in her chest. "Ma'am?"

"Maybe when you're out there in Colorado Springs next year, you can get one of the instructors to teach you how to make a decent cup of coffee."

# 45

## JAY

*Three months later, just before Thanksgiving*

*New York City*

Hartwell Academy had a memorial day for Cassie and Tim. Many people said very nice things about them, and there were lots of tears. There was also the announcement of a new scholarship by Tim's parents. The school was working with Em to bring ten refugees to Hartwell Academy every year, tuition free.

By all accounts, Ben Ando, Cassie's dad, had no knowledge of any of the proceedings in the Patrice Mixtos case. The company had hundreds of complaints in the courts at any given time, and Mr. Ando left the litigation end of the business to his attorneys.

After Cassie's death, Mr. Ando announced that Ando Chemical Inc. was divesting from all companies that posed health or infrastructure risks. The company's stock price dropped 70 percent. Mr. Ando was being forced off the company's board of directors. He said he planned to devote his time and money to the research and development of nontoxic pesticides and fertilizers. The name of his new company was going to be called Cassandra Endeavors. He moved Reeva Powell's mother to a luxury nursing home in New Jersey, on the water with 24-7 care, and set up an account to pay all her bills. Nick Sokolov was promoted to captain of Mr. Ando's new B550.

Jay met Brandon after school on Hartwell Academy's caged-in roof court. They shot hoops for a bit and then headed downstairs to the Astroturf field behind the school. They watched the last half hour of Em's field hockey practice. It was warm for late November. Warm and sunny.

Jay never felt he'd fully connected with the crowd at Hartwell—that was no surprise to him. The kids weren't mean or bullying. They were the opposite actually—helpful, friendly. But they were from a different world. The things they talked about—their skiing vacations in France, their parents' companies, their investment portfolios—Jay had no connection to these things. The big surprise was that Brandon and Emily didn't really fit in at Hartwell either, not anymore.

The hijacking had made the three of them very careful about where they focused their energy. Mostly they focused it on one another. They were a band of three, disconnected from the rest of the school. Who could relate to them after what they had been through? Yes, all kids probably have some kind of trauma in their past, Jay suspected, but being the victim of a hijacking was a very specific kind of terror. The things that had happened up there, the things they'd seen, the things they'd had to do . . .

Jay had nightmares about it: killing Tony. He kept seeing the oxygen tank spinning through the air, end over end, toward Tony's face. Sometimes the nightmares would creep into his waking life, in daydreams during geometry, on quiz day when the room was quiet and outside the window he'd watch the planes head away from the city, west.

He and Brandon had become close. They didn't talk much, but they didn't need to. Just being around each other was a comfort. They'd play video games for hours, multiplayer online games, where they could be on the same team. They stayed away from anything gory. Mostly they played car-racing games or the kind where you have to find treasure or build something or figure out a mystery.

The mystery.

Would they be able to get past what had happened up in the air a few months ago? Would the nightmares ever stop?

A group of girls came over to the bleachers. They invited Brandon and Jay to a party that was going down Saturday night. Brandon said thanks, he'd think about it. After the girls left, he said to Jay, "I keep thinking I hear her calling out to me, but when I turn around, she's not there of course." He wrote a lot about her, about Cassie. Jay pushed him to turn his journaling into a memoir and try to get it published, but Brandon said he had no interest, that the writing was for him, for Cassie. He said it was the one way he could still talk to her, or at least it felt that way, that she was somehow still here, listening.

Field hockey practice ended, and Emily stopped by the bleachers before heading inside with the team. "Give me ten minutes to put the equipment away, and I'll meet you guys out front."

Being manager of the field hockey team was yet another thing Emily had taken on. She never felt she was doing enough, and keeping busy was her way of not having to think about the hijacking. Jay would go with her to the soup kitchen on Sunday afternoons. The person who ran the kitchen knew Em's mom and kept trying to put Emily in a leadership role, managing the other volunteers, and then out front, serving the homeless, because she had such a great smile, but Emily was more comfortable in the back of the kitchen, she said, working the dishwasher station, where she could be alone.

The three of them headed for the train out to Queens. Em wanted to stop off and grab some flowers for Jay's mom.

Mrs. Rhee had laid out quite a spread for dinner—Italian food, which was Jay's favorite—pasta, lasagna, fried potatoes. When his mom went into the kitchen to get the dessert, Emily went with her.

Brandon rubbed his stomach and sighed. "I never leave here hungry," he said.

But he still looked hungry. He'd lost weight, and there was something hollow in his eyes. He stared out the window, toward the apartment building across the breezeway, but he seemed to be looking through it, not really seeing anything. He squinted like he was trying to get a glimpse of something far, far away, at the edge of the horizon and fading. "Jay, do you think I'll ever be able to stop thinking about her? To stop hoping that my phone's going to blip with a text, and Cassie's picture is going to pop up in the ID panel? You know that selfie, where she's hanging upside down on the climbing wall?"

Jay remembered it, just like he remembered seeing her hanging on to Brandon as he hung upside down from the slackline.

After dinner, the three of them cleaned up the kitchen while Mom got the card table ready. They played some game she learned at her church. She really got into it, the kind of game where speed counted, and you were always trying to slap one card on top of another. Jay couldn't figure out the rules, but it made him happy to see his mom play it. She smiled a lot more now. She'd gotten her tooth fixed—on a deep discount, of course. A new friend from church was a dental hygienist. They went to the movies sometimes. Mom was definitely putting herself out there a lot more these past few months.

The hijacking had shaken her as much as it had shaken Jay— shaken her awake. She'd realized that her entire life to that point had been lived for her son, despite Jay's begging her to take care of herself. She knew now that she had to do exactly that: to open herself up and give her heart to the world. Jay wondered if someday he'd be able to do the same, to put himself out there and meet new people and seek new adventures. If that was possible, it felt a long way off. Right now he wanted to keep his head down and hang back with Emily and Brandon, and when they weren't around, being alone felt good too.

After cards Mom excused herself to bed. She had to work the early shift the next day. The crew of three played Minecraft for a while, until the air traffic pattern shifted with the late November wind.

The planes were flying into LaGuardia directly over Jay's apartment—low too.

Low enough to make the windows clatter.

The three of them got quiet, and Jay realized he was as rattled as the windows. Em took his hand. Hers was warm and strong, and it fit just right.

"Stop thinking about it, you guys," she said.

"Right," Brandon said, sinking back into the couch.

Em turned to Jay. "This is gonna sound crazy, but if I sign up for a flamenco class, would you go with me? OMG, what is that thing on your lips?"

"What thing?" Jay said, wiping his mouth.

"Brand, do you see it? Jay's actually smiling." She slugged Jay's shoulder.

"Flamenco, huh?" Jay tried to picture himself doing it, and in the picture he looked ridiculous. "Yeah, Em, I'll go with you to your flamenco class."

"My hero," she said. She hugged him, and over her shoulder he saw Brandon tugging gently at the yellow rubber bracelet Cassie used to wear, the one that said *PEACE*.

# ACKNOWLEDGMENTS

With thanks to . . .

Scott Smith, Elizabeth Hill, Angie Smith-Hill, and Annie Kim, for their friendship;

Jodi, Alec, David, Emily, Bess, Lizette, Antonio, Josh, Yaffa, Morgan, the West brothers, and all the Scholastic angels, for their kindness;

Jeff Smith, for taking the time to speak with me and for his many years of service as a US Air Force and private jet pilot; Trevor Hoest, a fantastic pilot, also a fantastic nephew;

My amazing and amazingly generous editors: the fabulous Becky Shapiro Herrick, for getting it started; my pal Nan Mercado, superheroine and one of the nicest people I've ever known, for seeing it through; the absolutely awesome Erin Black for being totally nuts about adventure stories, not to mention dogs; and the spectacular Jody Corbett for bringing it home.

## ABOUT THE AUTHOR

Paul Griffin is the critically acclaimed author of many novels, including *Ten Mile River*, *The Orange Houses*, *Stay with Me*, *Burning Blue*, and *Adrift*, as well as the middle grade novels *When Friendship Followed Me Home* and *Saving Marty*. Paul lives in Manhattan with his family. He can be found online at paulgriffinstories.com.